The Sea Turtle

A Novel

Greg M. Dodd

HARVEST
CHRONICLES

Copyright © 2023 Greg M. Dodd
Published by Harvest Chronicles, an imprint of Rolos Tuesday.
www.gregmdodd.com

ISBN-13: 978-0-9915332-8-2 Paperback
Rolos Tuesday, Columbia, SC
Printed in the United States of America

ACKNOWLEDGMENTS

The chapter titles found in this book are from popular songs of the late 1960s and early 1970s. A Spotify playlist in chapter order is available for your listening pleasure. Just scan the QR code below. Enjoy.

"Summers are a gift."
- Sally Marie Fox

CONTENTS

INTRODUCTION

My name is Thomas Ransom Fox, Jr. My dad, Thomas Ransom Fox, Sr., went by his first name, Thomas, or Tom. My parents decided to call me Ransom to avoid any confusion around the house. My mother thought two Toms were one too many. My nickname is Ran. Ran Fox. No jokes, please. As you can imagine, I've spent most of my life correcting schoolteachers, bank tellers, doctors, clients, and everyone else who, by default, address me as Thomas or Tom. Thanks, Mom and Dad.

Ransom is a name that carries some significance in our family history. The story involves my father's grandfather's uncle on his father's side. That would be my first cousin, three times removed; I think that's how that works. Anyway, in the late 1800s, he left his family's home in the Low Country of South Carolina to live for a short time in England. While there, he met and married a woman from a small town called Bury Saint Edmunds. Her maiden name was Ransom. After moving back to the States, they had a son and named him Ransom Augustus Fox. He was the first Fox to earn a living doing something other than growing beans, corn, or milking cows. Around the turn of the century, he opened a general store and butcher shop about seventy miles north of Charleston in a small town called Georgetown. He ran it until 1934 when he died of typhus fever. There's a Circle K there now. Ransom Augustus Fox is seen as the originating carrier of a mythical entrepreneurial gene that's been passed down through the men in my family. The RAF gene, we call it. My grandfather had it. My own father claimed it. But as far as I can tell, it skipped me.

As I write this, I'm thirty-two years old, and I'm an attorney by trade. I'm married and have a three-year-old son, Tommy (yes, he's Thomas Ransom Fox, III). I talk with my wife frequently about how we can give our son a memorable childhood. Perhaps it's a thinly veiled effort on my part to give him something I didn't have. Most people close to me know that my memory of childhood is like a block of Swiss cheese. There are lots of holes in it. And some holes are pretty big. For instance, I don't remember being in kindergarten. Or first grade. (Now that I think about it, add second grade to the list.) Whenever a cousin or an old friend begins to share a funny story about something we supposedly did back in the day, I usually just nod and laugh as if I knew what the heck they were talking about. And while I've seen a picture of my nine-year-old self at Walt Disney World in 1971, I honestly don't remember being there. And that was way before Photoshop, so I'm pretty sure that's really me with the Mickey Mouse ears and purple snow cone standing in front of Dumbo the Flying Elephant. My dad must have taken the picture because he wasn't in it. Or, for all I know, he wasn't there.

My wife's favorite explanation for all this is that the aliens who abducted me when I was eleven (she's joking) accidentally erased all my pre-abduction social memories. Maybe, but I doubt it. I think it's more likely that my subconscious threw all those memories into a cardboard box, taped it shut, and tossed it into the attic of my mind for whatever psychoanalytic reasons work best.

But some random things from those days I do remember. Like my big fight with Lucas Brown after school in third grade. Or the little, blonde, horse-obsessed girl who sat next to me in fourth grade. I've forgotten what class we were in, but I do remember watching her draw elaborate pictures of horses on her assignment sheets instead of doing the work on them. And her name was Whinny. Seriously. You can't make up stuff like that.

And then there were the Donaldson twins, Frank and Finley. For elementary school kids, they were pretty intimidating. One of them was meaner than the other, but I never knew which one it was. They used to take turns pushing me down at recess. Or maybe it was the same one every time; I can't be sure. But I learned that if I just lay there like a dead possum, they really had no other ideas and would leave me alone. One of them, probably the nicer of the two, actually came to my dad's funeral last year.

Thomas Ransom Fox, Sr., passed away on June 2nd, 1993, from complications related to a heart attack at the age of 61, just like his father did in 1962. But the real cause of my father's death was set years earlier when he opened his own coffee shop. He worked fourteen hours a day, seven days a week while ignoring his health for 27 years. The RAF gene has its consequences. And he finally succumbed to them.

I used to hate coffee. Not the taste of it, just the fact that it exists. When I was growing up it seemed that coffee was the biggest rival for my dad's time and attention. And I always lost. He missed most of my activities during the school year and didn't have time for much else. The ultimate defeat came when I was 12. My father sent me away for the summer to stay with my aunt Sarah and uncle Breland at their rickety old beach house on the coast of South Carolina. A three-mile-long strip of white sand called Pawleys Island. Coffee had won. Or so I thought at the time.

That was the summer of 1974. And I remember every detail of it.

T. Ransom Fox, Jr.
July 4th, 1994
Pawleys Island, SC

ONE

Summer Breeze

My mother liked to say summers are a gift. From whom, to whom, I never really understood. But when I was a kid, any June morning that carried the promise of a warm breeze and sunshine would find me kicking off my covers, the excitement of a carefree day lifting me joyfully out of bed. But on this third Saturday morning of June, I lay in my favorite Snoopy pajamas gazing blankly out my bedroom window, my sheet pulled up to my chin. My eyes had opened much earlier than usual, and I couldn't go back to sleep. I watched the dawn slowly illuminate the live oak tree in our backyard and my rusting swing set beneath it. I felt like something in my life was about to change. It was an uneasy feeling, like my first day at Hand Middle School the prior September, only worse. At least I knew a little about what school had in store for me back then. Hallways full of noisy kids, the Donaldson twins, unfamiliar teachers, and the chaos of an all-too-short recess. But I had no idea what this day would bring. I wished the sun would just slow down.

I could hear my mother in her bedroom sorting through the large pile of shoes, sandals, and boots in her tiny closet. Our house, a one-story brick bungalow, was built around the time my dad was born in the early 1930s. It was in a nice, quiet, tree-lined neighborhood called Shandon, one of the first suburbs of Columbia, South Carolina. But my mom liked to say the homes, and the closets within them, must have been designed by architects whose wives didn't have a lot of shoes.

I always thought of my mom as a neat, orderly, somewhat frugal person. But when it came to footwear, none of that applied. I'm willing to bet she had two hundred pairs of shoes in that little closet. OK, maybe a little less than that, but still.

And as part of her early-morning-getting-dressed routine, she'd get on her hands and knees and dig around trying to find the right matching pair for the day.

The thumping sound against my wall, a few inches from my pillow, had been going on longer than usual. That would rule out boots, I thought, as they were the easiest to find. And we were going to be in the car for a couple of hours, so that would rule out any need for platforms. My bet, as I lay there, was on tennis shoes or sandals. She had lots of sandals, which may explain the prolonged thumping, which suddenly stopped.

A moment later, my mother opened my bedroom door, knocking as she entered. "Wake up, Ran," she said, sporting a pair of shiny, red, opened-toed sandals. "We need to get on the road, soon."

"I am awake," I said, turning my attention back toward the yard.

"Well then, how about you get out of bed?"

I lay motionless, my eyes gazing out the window. "Why'd y'all give me that swing set?" I asked, rolling over to face her.

"What do you mean?" she asked. Her hands were on her hips as she took stock of my toys and recently worn clothes scattered across the floor. "It was a birthday present, silly. When you were five." She bent over to pick up an astronaut-clad GI Joe from the floor. "Or six," she added. "I can't remember."

"How come every time I tried to swing on it, you'd call me inside to eat or clean something? It's like you didn't want me on it."

"You're imagining things," she said, tossing the GI Joe into my toy chest in the closet. She picked up a sample of my clothes. "Are these clean or dirty?"

I ignored her question and stayed on topic. "And Dad was always too busy to swing on it with me."

Holding up two shirts and a pair of mismatched socks, she dismissed my commentary on misplaced parental priorities and cast her trademark, one-eyebrow-raised glare in my direction.

"Dirty," I guessed, before continuing my unfocussed whining. "Now, you're sending me away where I won't see it for three months."

Dropping the shirts and socks back onto the floor, she began pushing the rest of my clothes into a pile with her feet. "First of all, it's not for three months. It's two. Or two and a half. And, you haven't been on that swing in ages. Why are you worried about it now?"

"I'm too old to play on it, and it just sits there looking at me."

"Too old? You're twelve, for heaven's sake."

"I'm almost thirteen," I reminded her.

She waved her hands in the air, classic Mom body language for *I'm through talking about this.* "Why are we even talking about this?" she asked for good measure. "Get up, so we can get you ready to leave."

The arrangements had all been made without my consent. It was my dad's idea. I imagined him saying something like this to my mother:

> *How 'bout we let my cranky old brother, Breland,*
> *look after our kid this summer? What's his name*
> *again? Ran? Anyway, I've got coffee to sell.*

OK, so my twelve-year-old imagination could be a bit hyperbolic at times, but the sentiment seemed plausible to me at the time. And, while I hadn't voiced my opinion about being exiled – not that I was asked for my thoughts on the matter – I *really* didn't want to go. So, I figured it was time to show my hand. I pushed myself up on my pillow, crossed my arms, and looked squarely at my mother. "Mom," I said firmly, "I don't want to go to the beach." That should do it, I thought. A vision of a summer at home with my two-year-old, brown and white Springer Spaniel, Pepper, flashed before my eyes.

"Well, you're going," she said while looking under my desk for more clothes.

Apparently, when you're twelve, you don't have much leverage in these types of negotiations. So, I scrambled to think of something else while she continued.

"And you're going to have fun," she assured me, pulling some underwear from under my desk. "Now, start getting your things together. I have to be back here by three o'clock this afternoon for that choir thing at the church, so let's get moving."

"But there's nothing to do at the beach," I moaned, now playing the sympathy card. "Plus, I don't know anybody." I gave her my best sad face, with the forlorn eyes and everything.

"You know your aunt Sarah and your uncle Breland."

It would be four years before Gary Coleman would give us "Whatchu talkin' 'bout, Willis?" But that's basically the look I gave her.

"What's that look for?" she asked.

I didn't feel like explaining the fact that twelve-year-old boys don't hang out with old people, particularly my uncle Breland, and call it fun. So, I just sighed and rolled over to face the window again. The sun had ignored my wish and was quickly casting shadows across my backyard. I was almost ready to give up.

"Maybe you'll make a new friend," my mom posed. "You know, a beach friend. Think of it as a great opportunity, Ran. Summers are a gift."

There it was. I was waiting for that. I rolled back to face her and offered a counter, "How about I share that gift with a friend from here? They could go with me." My hope for a fun summer suddenly had new life. How could she say no to a perfect compromise?

"No," she said.

I growled and pulled the covers over my head in frustration.

"Honey, I can't just ask one of your friends' mothers if I could borrow their son for three months. Or two and a half, whatever."

I felt a quick release of adrenaline. She had made her first mistake, and I jumped all over it. "You're letting Uncle Breland and Aunt Sarah borrow *me* for three months," I countered. I had done it. I had her cornered. What could she possibly say now?

"Well, that's different. Now, get up and get your stuff together. We need to get on the road."

Life lesson number one: When negotiating, grown-ups play by different rules. I decided to stall for more time. "Where's Dad?" I asked.

"You know the answer to that. Now get up."

She clapped her hands twice like she does when she calls Pepper. I guess it was supposed to have the same effect on me. But I knew there was no treat in the waiting.

Straightforward negotiations had failed, so I decided to try the time-tested kid approach: Complain until you wear your poor mom down. "But why do I have to stay with Uncle Breland and Aunt Sarah?" I asked.

Pepper walked into my room with an expectant look on his face.

My mom sighed, dropped her shoulders, and looked directly at me. "We've been through this, honey," she said. "Your dad is swamped with the café, like always, and I've got my hands full taking care of your grandma. Besides, this will be good for you."

"But what about a—"

"And we can't afford a babysitter."

"Well, why can't I just stay here by myself?"

"Not gonna happen."

"But I don't like Uncle Breland."

"Ransom, that's not nice. He's family."

"Well, I don't. He smells like cigarettes, and he calls me names."

"Oh, he does not."

"He does too!" I argued. "When he was here for Dad's birthday last year, he called me 'Oompa-Loompa' the whole time."

I always liked my mom's laugh, even when she was laughing at me.

"That's just Uncle Breland, honey," she said, still chuckling. "He's got a nickname for everybody. Now, get up and get your things together."

Despite my best efforts, she had won. I had nothing else. "Yes, ma'am," I said in defeat. But I stayed under the covers just the same, as a final, pointless show of passive defiance.

"We can stop by the coffee shop," she offered, "and say goodbye to your father if you want."

"No, that's OK." After all, I thought, he didn't say goodbye to me; why should I say goodbye to him?

"Oh, come on. He'd enjoy that. Maybe he'll let you try some coffee."

"I hate coffee," I said. I had never tasted coffee, but I knew I wouldn't like it. I didn't want to like it.

"Suit yourself," she said as she turned to leave my room. "We're leaving in twenty minutes."

When it came to getting ready to go somewhere, twenty minutes to my mom was more like forty-five minutes in real life. So, I had no reason to rush. I knew I'd be waiting on her, not the other way around. I swung my feet off my bed and onto my new red, white, and blue shag carpet. Yes, I really had red, white, and blue shag carpet in my room. It was 1974, after all. A time when designers of clothes, architecture, cars, and home décor seemed to be on one collective acid trip. My mother had made the mistake of letting me pick out the carpet and colors for my room. And with the country's bicentennial coming up, looking patriotic seemed like the radical thing to do. But the carpet's three colors bled together to form what looked like a ten-by-twelve pool of purple vomit. The carpet was meant to go with my blue walls. Again, I blame my mother for trusting a twelve-year-old.

I took a quick inventory of my clothes, those my mom missed on the floor of my closet and those in my dresser. I stuffed a few t-shirts, shorts, underwear, and a bathing suit into a small duffle bag I found in the back of my closet and crammed everything else into the pillowcase I borrowed from my bed. "I'm ready!" I called out to my mother, just two minutes after she'd left my room.

"OK, give me just a minute," she answered from her bedroom.

I walked down the hall to the den and petted Pepper until he got tired of the attention and left me alone on the couch. I got up, hopped over the coffee table, and turned on our Zenith floor-model color TV. There were no remote controls back then, but since there were only four channels to choose from there wasn't much flipping around. I turned the plastic dials to channel 10, then 19, then 25, but my Saturday morning cartoons weren't on yet. *Speed Buggy* came on at 8:00, followed by *Bugs Bunny/Road Runner* at 8:30. But the clock above the mantle said it wasn't even seven o'clock. I found *The World at War* on ETV, but I wasn't in the mood. World War II was interesting, but I had my own problems.

Feeling a bit hungry, I turned off the TV and wandered through the dining room and into the kitchen, followed by Pepper. There was only one thing in the pantry meant solely for me: Captain Crunch with Crunch Berries. I poured myself a bowl, added some whole milk, and began crunching loud enough to wake up the neighbors. While I guided my spoon around my bowl hunting for red crunch berries, I tried to help the Captain find the shortest route to the hidden treasure on the back of the cereal box. My mom came in before I could finish.

"You're still in your pajamas?" she asked.

I guess I was. I forgot to put on real clothes when I was getting ready. "I'll change in a second," I answered, my mouth full of cereal as I searched for the treasure.

"At least you're eating. Hurry up and finish," she said, digging through her purse on the counter. "And then go brush your teeth. Did you already pack your toothbrush?"

Of course not. No twelve-year-old worries about tooth decay or bad breath. But I didn't say that. "No, ma'am," I said, instead.

"And don't forget to take your summer reading assignment to the beach with you. You need to have that finished when I come back in August to get you."

I tried to pretend I didn't hear that last comment. My school was making us read *Where the Red Fern Grows* over the summer. But giving up my free time to read something other than a comic book was the last thing I wanted to do. So, I stayed focused on my breakfast and hoped she would go away if I ignored her.

"Ran?" she asked, as she put the things she took out of her purse back in her purse.

I put on my best deep-thought scowl as I studied the back of the cereal box.

"Ransom? Did you hear me?"

She wasn't going away. I disengaged from the treasure hunt, forced a sighing yes from my chest, and put another spoonful of cereal in my mouth.

"OK, then. Hurry up."

I finished my cereal in two large slurps from the bowl, then headed down the hall to take care of my teeth. After a quick brushing, I stuffed my toothpaste, wet toothbrush, and *Where the Red Fern Grows* into my pillowcase and carried everything to the kitchen. My mom was waiting and ready to go. I had underestimated her.

"You're not going in pajamas, now go change."

I would have gotten around to putting on clothes eventually, but as Pepper entered the kitchen, I saw an opportunity to salvage something from my failed morning protest. "Why can't I go like this?" I asked, as serious as I could be.

"I'm not dropping you off at your aunt's house in pajamas."

"Well...if I go change, will you let Pepper ride with us?" I could tell my mom was getting frustrated; it was working.

"For heaven's sake," she huffed. She looked at me, then at Pepper.

Pepper smiled back and wagged his tail. Good dog, Pepper. Mom always was a sucker for his big brown eyes.

"Yes," she finally said. "Just please go get dressed."

If you're keeping score at home, that would make it Mom 3, Ran 1. But at least I'm on the board. I ran down the hall to change out of my pajamas, with Pepper chasing behind me. "You wanna go for a ride?" I asked him. Those words would always give Pepper a big case of the zoomies. He began running up and down the hallway, sliding past my bedroom door with that maniacal look on his face, then racing back to the front of the house where he'd turn the den rug into a wrinkled heap. I smiled for the first time that morning. But it was time to leave.

TWO

I'm a Believer

My mom drove a 1968 Chevy Chevelle station wagon. It was hunter green with black vinyl bench seats, front and back, a push-button AM/FM radio, and factory air conditioning. When the back seat was folded down, my friends and I would use the open cargo space as a mobile playroom for my GI Joes. Whenever my mom took a turn, we'd slide or roll from side to side on the painted metal surface working the action into our war games. I know what you're thinking: Seat belts. The car had them, the kind that just buckled across your lap. But wearing them was, well, optional back then. It was a much simpler, less responsible time.

I tossed my bags into the car and started to climb in the back with Pepper, who'd been sitting there by himself patiently waiting for us to leave, but my mom wanted me to ride in the front with her. We didn't get two blocks from our house before Pepper jumped over the seat to ride with me. He sat between us for a moment and looked out the windshield, then climbed onto my lap and hung his head out the window. But it wasn't long before he just balled up on the seat and went to sleep.

For the first thirty minutes or so, I played with the radio and didn't talk. I liked to turn the knob and hunt for good songs. If I heard someone talking, it was on to the next channel.

"Just leave it on one station, please," my mom huffed.

Maybe that's how they did it back in the old days, but this was 1974. We had three FM music stations to choose from in Columbia, not to mention a couple on AM. So why just sit on one station, when there was a whole world of music out there? My favorite station was WCOS 1400 AM. They played all the Top 40 stuff, but my mom said AM radio was too "buzzy." She preferred some elevator music station at 105 on the FM dial. Yawn. But despite my mom's request, I kept the dial moving. And thanks to my timely knob turning, we had already heard *Dancing Machine* by the Jackson 5 three times before we'd even turned off the Sumter Highway. But the Columbia stations began to turn into static around Pineview, so my mom turned off the radio. With Pepper asleep and nothing to listen to, I just stared out my window at the gradually flattening landscape of eastern South Carolina. My mom tried to make conversation, but I wasn't interested. Actually, I was just trying to make her feel bad for letting Dad send me to the beach. And I had learned early in life that grunts are a very effective way to kill unwanted conversation, and I used them strategically.

"What's your friend Will doing this summer?" my mom asked.

Grunt.

"Do you know if his mother started working?"

Grunt.

"So, which movie did you like better: *Herbie Rides Again* or *The Love Bug*?"

Grunt.

"Oh!" she shouted. "Six!"

"What?" I asked, caught off guard.

"We gave you the swing set for your *sixth* birthday," she said. "Whew! That was really bugging me."

Grunt.

By the time we reached Manning an hour into our trip, she had stopped trying. Other than Pepper occasionally demanding attention or wanting to look out the window, we rode in silence until we hit the "nine-mile curve" halfway between Andrews and Georgetown. We were just thirty minutes from the beach. The approaching reality of my summer began to rustle the anxiety in my chest. So, I decided to break my silence.

"What if Uncle Breland is so mean to me that I want to come home?" I asked.

"Oh, so you can talk now," my mom said, cutting her eyes at me.

"Seriously, what if he, like, locks me in a closet or something?"

"Locks you in a closet," she said flatly as she turned her head toward me with raised eyebrows.

"Yeah," I said, with confidence, nodding my head.

Pepper lifted his head and looked at me.

"It's possible," I said to both of them.

"Honey, if I thought for one second that you'd be in some sort of danger down here, I wouldn't be driving you to their house. Besides, if you have any problems, talk to your aunt Sarah. She can call me if she needs to."

My aunt Sarah was a nice old woman. How she ever got stuck being married to my uncle Breland was a mystery to me. I still wasn't sure how the whole marriage thing worked, anyway. I knew that people were supposed to fall in love with each other. I knew that from all the songs I heard on the radio. For example, just two days before, I stayed up late at Will Mason's end-of-the-school-year sleepover and watched Olivia Newton-John sing *If You Love Me [Let Me Know]* on *The Midnight Special*. Wolfman Jack was hosting. Halfway through the song, she turned her head and cast a longing, blue-eyed gaze directly into the TV camera. She was staring straight at me. My mouth dropped open. "Oh, my god," I remember saying out loud as I locked eyes with Olivia. That's it, I thought. That's what love feels like. But whenever I was around old married people, I never saw anything like that. And I didn't have an older brother or sister to annoy about it, so my only lessons on love came from songs on the radio.

Hooked on a Feeling, by Blue Swede

Could it be I'm Falling in Love, by The Spinners

Diamond Girl, by Seals & Crofts

Let Me Be There, by my new girlfriend, Olivia Newton-John

The Air That I Breathe, by…somebody, I can't remember.

Let's Get It On, by Marvin Gaye

I admit I didn't know what that last song was really about until I was in my teens, but you get my point.

Maybe old people just didn't have good music when they were young. I only knew that when I got my chance at love, I was not going to end up like Uncle Breland. Or my dad, for that matter. Which raised an obvious question in my mind.

"Mom?"

"I'm right here, honey," she said without taking her eyes off the road.

"When you met Dad, did you know you were gonna marry him?"

She chuckled lightly and gave me a quizzical look. "Where did *that* come from?"

"I was just wondering…how all that stuff works."

"What stuff?"

"You know…love and stuff."

"Love, huh?" she asked with suspicion in her voice and a smile on her face as she stared straight ahead.

"Yeah. You know…"

"This isn't about Chrissy Castle again, is it?"

"What? No!" My loud denial woke Pepper from his nap. He looked around to get his bearings then placed his muzzle on my leg. "And it's Cissy, not Chrissy."

"Oh. Excuse me," she said, not hiding the smirk on her face.

I had made the mistake of mentioning Cissy once last fall. She had just moved from Alabama and sat in front of me in math class. I'd made a habit of staring at her blonde ponytail and daydreaming about her turning around to talk to me. It never happened. But I'm sure the distraction cost me a letter grade.

"Never mind," I said, feeling defeated. "I'm sorry I even asked." I kept my eyes on the passing corn fields and wondered why it was so hard to talk to grown-ups about anything. After a moment, my mother broke the silence.

"When I met your father," she started, "I was on a date with someone else."

She had my full attention. But I said nothing, afraid I would steer her off-topic.

"We were at a party when I was a sophomore in college. The boy I was with was someone I had been out with a couple times before. I liked him, but it was nothing serious." She paused for a moment. "Oh my gosh," she added.

"What?" I asked.

"I can't remember his name."

"Who cares, what about Dad?"

She shook her head. "Right, your dad. So, there were a lot of people there." She paused for a moment and leaned toward her steering wheel. "Hang on a sec." She put on her left blinker and accelerated past a pick-up truck full of old tires poking along in front of us. When she had settled back into our lane and checked her mirrors, she continued. "It was a sorority thing. The party, I mean. It was at the old Women's Club on Blossom Street. You know, where you had your Boy Scouts meetings?"

"Don't remind me," I said, trying to repress my brief time as a scout. Structured group activities requiring uniforms apparently weren't my thing. And a merit badge just wasn't enough incentive for me to give up Saturday morning cartoons for wood carving or coin collecting.

"Anyway, my date," my mom continued. "Shoot, what was his name?"

"Mom."

"Sorry, that's going to bug me."

"Can it bug you later? We're almost to the beach."

"Sure. Anyway...where was I?"

"I have no idea."

"Oh! So, my date went to the restroom and left me standing by myself. But a friend of mine named Jan...Why can I remember her name but not the guy I went there with?"

I huffed loud enough to make my point.

"Sorry, so Jan came walking up with her date to say hello."

"And she was with Dad?" I guessed.

"Yes, she was," she said. "She introduced us." A smile grew on her face as she lost herself in the memory. "He was quite handsome, your father."

I watched her as she stared down the road ahead. "And that's when you knew?" I asked, snapping her out of her trance.

"Knew what?" she asked, back with me again.

"That you were going to marry him."

She laughed. "Goodness, no." She shook her head. "That took a while."

"Why?"

"Because love doesn't work like that."

I didn't want to believe her. "But I thought–"

"Honey, you don't just look at someone and fall head-over-heels in love with them. There's another word for that."

I didn't like what I was hearing. I thought love was supposed to be magical, like some spell cast over you. Olivia Newton-John wouldn't lie to me.

"Love takes time," she added.

"Maybe for you," I replied, unfiltered. I looked away but felt my mom's eyes on me. As I turned my head, she gave me a half-hearted smile. I couldn't tell if I had hurt her feelings or if she just knew something I didn't. Or both.

"Well, let's just wait a few more years," she said, "and you can tell me if you think differently."

THREE

I Can Help

We'd been riding in silence since our discussion on love ended without resolution. In other words, my mom failed to see that I was right, and she was wrong. When we reached Georgetown, just thirteen miles from the beach, I rolled down my window so Pepper could get some fresh air, but the air wasn't fresh. It was warm, heavy, and smelled like the rotten hardboiled eggs my mom forgot to throw away after Easter. He hung his head out the window anyway.

"Why does it smell like that?" I asked.

"It's just the papermill, honey. That's where your uncle Breland used to work. He always said it smells like money."

"It smells like poop to me," I countered.

"Well, don't tell him that," she said. "He might lock you in a closet."

I gave her a look.

"I'm kidding!" she said with a laugh as she drove us into town. "Oh, see that brick building up on the right?"

I lifted myself higher on my seat so I could get a better view out of the windshield. Up ahead was a small, one-story brick building with large plate-glass windows across the front and a sign on top. "The barbershop?" I asked.

"Yep, that building belonged to your great, great, uncle, or someone like that. He's who you were named after."

"I thought I was named after Dad."

"You were, but your father told me a long time ago the name Ransom came from your great uncle. Or great, great uncle or cousin, I can't remember. Anyway, he owned a general store there back in the 30s, I think. Pretty groovy, huh?"

Grunt.

The rest of the drive through Georgetown took less than five minutes. It was a small town, the best part of which was the water surrounding it. As we crossed over the Pee Dee and Waccamaw rivers on our way out of town, I watched a small fishing boat glide effortlessly across the glassy, dark brown water. I wondered what it would be like to swim down there.

"Lots of alligators and snakes down there," my mom said, unprompted. Her mind-reading powers could be a little annoying at times.

Once we crossed the bridges, there wasn't anything else to look at for the next thirteen miles besides trees and a stray dog trotting alongside the highway. When I saw the dog, I gave a quick look at my mom.

"No," she said.

See what I mean?

We finally took a right turn off Highway 17 at a gas station and made our way over to the island. As we passed over a small bridge, I studied the green saltwater creek running through the marsh behind the island. "Are there snakes and alligators in there too?" I asked.

"No. Just sharks, stingrays, and a few jellyfish," she said, casually. "Oh, and you might cut your foot on an oyster shell if you're not careful."

I watched her face closely and waited for signs of a smirk. It took a second, but it finally appeared, so I called her bluff. "I guess next you're gonna tell me there's hungry bears roaming the island, right?"

"No," she answered, a smile growing on her face. "Just your uncle Breland."

"That's not funny," I said. She sure thought it was.

"I'm just kidding, honey. You'll be fine down here. Just be safe, stay out of the creek, and let your aunt and uncle look after you. OK?"

"Yes, ma'am," I answered. What else could I say at that point? I pulled Pepper onto my lap and held him up to the open window. The warm salty air made his brown nose twitch in all directions.

"That's their house up there on the left," she said pointing over the steering wheel.

Pawleys Island was just a collection of old wooden two-story houses, some bigger and nicer than others, sitting on either side of a two-lane road that meandered up and down the island. One or two rows of houses sat on the beach side; the rest kept watch over the creek with a few scattered in between. My mom said the newer houses, all up on stilts, were built in the years since Hurricane Hazel washed over the island back when she was in college. My uncle's house was one of those that survived the hurricane, exactly how I don't understand. As we approached, it looked like it could collapse at any minute. It was an unpainted, wood plank, two-story house that sat flush on the sandy ground beneath it. Screened porches fronted both levels, with a set of outside stairs leading up to the second floor. My aunt was making her way down them as we parked the car in front of the house.

"Hand me my purse, sweetie," my mom said. "It's there on the floor."

I moved Pepper over and handed my mom her purse. She placed it on her lap and dug around for a moment, then pulled out some cash.

"I meant to give this to you before we got here," she said. "Here's three five-dollar bills and five ones. That's twenty dollars. Make that last, OK?"

"Yes, ma'am," I said. I took the bills from her and put them in my pocket. "Thank you, ma'am."

"And don't spend that on candy or fireworks or anything silly like that," she said, ruling out the first two things that came to my mind.

My mom got out first, while I lingered with Pepper inside the car. Aunt Sarah gave my mom a hug as they exchanged hellos, then turned her attention to me.

"And who's this young man in the car?" she asked, stepping in my direction.

"Hey, Aunt Sarah," I said through the open window. "It's me, Ran," I added just to be sure. You can never tell if old people are joking sometimes.

"And I see you brought a friend with you."

"This is Pepper," I said. "You remember Pepper, don't you?"

"Why, sure I do." She reached out and scratched Pepper behind his ears. "Hello, sweety."

My mom quickly interrupted my aunt's communion with Pepper. "Ran, why don't you grab your things and take Pepper inside so I can talk with Aunt Sarah for a minute."

"Ran, honey," said Aunt Sarah, "you can put your things in the bedroom just to the right of the kitchen, upstairs."

"Yes, ma'am." I opened the car door and let Pepper jump out. "Come on, Pepper."

The fact that neither my mom nor my aunt said anything as Pepper and I made our way up the stairs and inside the house told me they wanted to talk about something I wasn't supposed to hear. So, of course, I was going to listen. I walked through the screen door, passed through the porch and into the den, but stopped just inside the door. I dropped my stuff, kicked off my flip-flops, and crawled on my stomach back out onto the porch so I could listen. Jonny Quest couldn't have done any better, I thought.

"So, how are you, Sarah?" I heard my mom ask.

I crawled a little closer to the screen between two rocking chairs so I could see them talking beside the car. Pepper crawled up close to me and put his head next to mine. "Shh, be quiet," I whispered to Pepper.

"I'm fine," my aunt said, shrugging her shoulders. "We're fine."

"Thank you again for looking after our boy," my mom said, rubbing Aunt Sarah's shoulder.

"Well, I hope he…" she said pausing. She turned to look up at the house.

I ducked my head. I don't think she saw me.

"I hope he enjoys his stay with us," Aunt Sarah continued.

"How's Breland been about all this?" I heard my mom ask. I lifted my head just in time to see Aunt Sarah turn and look up at the house again. I ducked.

"He's...I think it might be hard for him at first. I think that's why he's been gone all day. I'm not sure when he'll be back."

"Do you want me to stay until he gets home?"

"Oh, gosh, no. Ran's a good boy. We'll be fine."

"Well, please call me if you have any concerns. I'll be home later this evening."

"If I need anything, Sally, I'll be sure to call." (Sorry, I forgot to mention that my mom's name is Sally. Sally Marie Fox. OK, back to Aunt Sarah.) "But don't worry about us," assured my aunt. "We'll be fine."

"I had some second thoughts about this, you know," said my mom. "But Tom thinks it might help things."

"I think Tom's heart is in the right place," said Aunt Sarah. "Please thank him for me. We'll see what the Lord does with it."

OK, I had no idea what that was all about. Other than the fact that my dad wanted to get rid of me for the summer and Uncle Breland wasn't thrilled to have me around, my spying revealed nothing new.

"Ran," called my mom, looking up at the house. "Come on back down here so I can say goodbye."

I crawled backward on my stomach into the den before standing up. I stuck my head out the door. "Did you call for me, Mom?" I asked innocently.

"Bring Pepper back down. I've got to get back on the road."

Pepper walked with me to the porch screen door. "Can Pepper stay with me, Mom?"

"Uh..." my mom said, slowly. She looked at Aunt Sarah, then back up at me. "I need Pepper home with me this summer. Is that OK?"

I was disappointed, but not surprised with the answer. I started down the stairs with Pepper running ahead of me. He ran and jumped through the open car door onto the front seat as I shuffled over to my mom.

"You don't want me to be alone all summer, do you?" she asked, pulling me close with a one-arm hug.

"I was going to say the same to you," I said, seriously.

"Ah, funny boy," she said, rubbing her hand in my hair. "You be good, and don't bother your uncle."

"Yes, ma'am," I said, trying to fix my hair.

She gave Aunt Sarah a hug, said goodbye, then hugged me again, told me she loved me, etc., then got in the car, and drove away. Aunt Sarah and I watched her green station wagon roll down the street until she turned and was out of sight. We stood there for a moment without moving, our eyes still focused on the empty road leading away from the house. I felt my aunt's arm land gently around my shoulder. I looked up at her as she looked down at me. She gave me a slight, uncertain smile. I got the feeling we were both sorry to see my mom leave.

FOUR

You Ain't Seen Nothing Yet

My aunt seemed to be a few years older than my mom, both in how she acted and in her appearance. They were about the same height, but Aunt Sarah was a little round, without seeming overweight. While my mom had long, super-straight dark brown hair, my aunt's wavy light blonde hair formed a persistent poofy circle around her head. And she always wore dresses, the kind that looked like a blouse that narrowed at the waist but didn't stop until it got to her knees. I guess that was the style at some point, and she locked in on it. And she never wore shoes around the house. Ever. I liked that about her.

After watching my mom leave, we turned to go inside.

"Are you hungry?" she asked me.

I would come to learn that was my aunt's favorite non-sequitur. "Yes, ma'am," I answered.

"Well, let's get you something to eat. What would you like?"

"Do you have Captain Crunch with Crunch Berries?" I asked. I'd already had that for breakfast, but I was just curious to see what kind of place I was staying in.

"No, I don't have that," she said, as we walked up the stairs. The wooden planks beneath us creaked with every step. "How about a peanut butter and jelly sandwich?"

"I guess," I said, with a shrug. It was cliché kid food, but it would do.

"And since I knew you were coming," she said, "I have some fresh-baked chocolate chip cookies for dessert. How about that?"

"OK," I said, following Aunt Sarah onto the porch and into the den. The cookies weren't a bad start, but the specter of my uncle looming somewhere out there on the island still had me a little nervous. "Where's Uncle Breland?" I asked, browsing around the den.

"I think he's fishing down at the creek," she said. "He might be there a while, so I don't know when you'll see him."

No hurry, I thought. But that did remind me. "Are there sharks in the creek?" I asked. A little fact-checking never hurt.

"I've never seen any," she said, heading into the kitchen. "Make yourself comfortable, honey. I'll have your sandwich ready in a minute."

I plopped down on the green fabric couch facing the porch and TV. From the hard feel of it, I could tell it was one of those fold-out beds, the kind I slept on at Will Mason's party. The thought of sleeping in the den and watching late movies bounced around in my head. "Hey, Aunt Sarah," I called out toward the kitchen. "Can I watch TV?" *American Bandstand* might still be on, I thought. I just hoped it was better than last Saturday's show. Dick Clark had some guy I'd never heard of sing a hillbilly song called *I'm a Yo-Yo Man.* Yes, he was.

Aunt Sarah took a few steps into the den. "Oh, honey," she said, "that TV hasn't worked for a few months." She disappeared back into the kitchen.

My mouth hung open as my brain tried to process what just happened. She had pulled the pin, dropped the grenade, and walked out. No TV. No *American Bandstand.* No *Bugs Bunny.* No *Six Million Dollar Man.* No *All in the Family.* No *Partridge Family.* Well, that last one I could live without. But...no TV? All summer? I knew most shows were reruns in the summer, but that wasn't the point.

From the kitchen, she tried to explain. "A storm broke off the antenna on our roof back in March. Your uncle Breland just hasn't gotten around to fixing it, yet." She reappeared with a tray carrying my sandwich, a few cookies, and a glass of milk. "I'm sorry, honey." She placed my lunch on the coffee table in front of the sofa and went back into the kitchen to hide.

I gathered myself, as best I could, stood up, and walked slowly over to the TV. It looked older than the one we had at home. It sat on a table and was a lot smaller. I pulled the knob to turn it on and waited for something to appear. Once the screen warmed up, snow, as my mom called it, was all I saw. Zillions of black and white dots dancing around the screen making nothing but a static buzzing sound. I twisted the VHF and UHF channel changer knobs all the way around, twice, but nothing appeared. After standing there for a moment, in mourning, I turned it off.

I refused to eat lunch in front of a TV that wouldn't work, so I picked up my tray and took it out to the porch. I sat down in a rocking chair, balanced the tray on my lap, and began to eat, shaking my head. Since *March*, I thought. Sigh. But I have to say, the first few bites of my sandwich almost made me forget about the TV. My aunt made it with crunchy peanut butter, which I hadn't had on a PB&J before. My mom always bought the creamy kind, but crunchy was a game changer. And, to her credit, she used grape jam instead of jelly. It was the highlight of my day up to that point.

As I ate, I held my milk in one hand so I could rock back and forth in the chair, pushing off the wooden floor with my bare toes. A slight, persistent breeze blew in from the left, which would have been north. I could see the ocean in between the houses across the street and hear the waves rolling in. Besides the sound of a few kids screaming on the beach every now and then, and the occasional car or bike going by, it was very peaceful. For a twelve-year-old, that would usually translate into boring, but it wasn't that bad. My aunt Sarah joined me halfway through my sandwich.

"Your uncle Breland loves it out here on the porch," she said, sitting down in the rocking chair next to me. "It's so peaceful."

"Yes, ma'am," I said, my mouth full.

In lieu of forcing awkward conversation with an old person, I worked on finishing my sandwich. While I ate, Aunt Sarah rocked slowly back and forth in her chair, humming something quietly to herself. She did seem to take joy in just sitting there. But I needed a little more stimulation.

"So, what do people do around here?" I asked, taking the last bite of my sandwich. "Besides, you know, sitting on the porch."

She took her time before answering. "Well, if I were your age," she said, "I think I would be playing on the beach." She looked over at me and smiled softly. "After you finish your cookies, why don't you head down there?"

"By myself?" I asked. I didn't know if that was allowed.

"Just don't go in the water without anyone watching you," she said. "I promised your mother, OK?"

"Yes, ma'am," I said, preparing myself to get up. "Can I eat my cookies after I come back from the beach?"

She nodded as she rocked forward. "They'll be in the kitchen for you."

"Thank you, ma'am!" I got up quickly, leaving my tray of cookies on the chair. As I stepped toward the screen door, the sight of all the houses between us and the beach made me stop. "How do I get down there?" I asked.

"Just find a path between the houses," she said. "Once you get down there, you'll see."

"OK, thanks!"

Without bothering to put on my flip-flops, I made my way quickly down the stairs to the street. Turning left, I began walking north, keeping my eyes peeled for an opening across the street that led to the beach. The pea gravel asphalt was hot in the midday sun, so I kept my bare feet in the sand beside the pavement.

More of the houses across the street seemed like the newer kind my mom talked about. They were raised up on stilts and had all been painted. Light shades of blue, yellow, gray, or green seemed to be the only colors available. And they all had names. "Who names a house?" I wondered as I walked. Aunt Sarah's house had no name that I was aware of. But I passed by *The Brown Pelican, The Gray Man, Surf & Turf,* and my favorite, *The Beach House.* Underneath each were cars, station wagons, bicycles, fishing boats, and piles of folded beach chairs.

About four or five houses down, I found a narrow sandy path between two rows of houses that led straight toward the beach. I looked back at the house to see if Aunt Sarah was watching but couldn't see her on the porch. I trotted across the street to the other side and headed up the path, excited about what I would find. Who would be out there? Would I see any kids my age? What does everybody do out there?

My mom said we stayed at Uncle Breland's house once, before I started kindergarten and before my dad opened the café, but I didn't remember any of it. So, essentially, this was about to be my first time on a beach.

I'd only gone about ten yards down the path before I felt something like tiny needles stabbing both of my feet. I dropped to the ground on my rear end and found several little round sticker things clinging to the bottom of each foot. They were like tiny little landmines with spikes. If I had known any good cuss words back then, I may have let a few rip. In addition to the pain, I was a little irritated that my aunt didn't warn me about these. What other little torture traps lurked in the sand ahead? I gently pulled each one loose, rubbed the bottom of my feet, and checked the ground around me before getting up.

I continued up the path with caution, my eyes scanning the ground carefully before each step. After reaching the tall dunes guarding the beach, I scurried upwards, my feet sliding into the loose sand as I pushed myself to the top. Allowing myself to feel excited for the first time that day, I stood on the dunes like an explorer who'd just discovered a new world.

About two hundred yards to my right, a long wooden pier stretched out into the ocean. At its end, men with long fishing poles dangled their lines in the water below. Scattered across the beach were women lying on towels or sitting in chairs reading books. Little kids dug holes in the sand and a few people walked north or south along the shoreline. Out in the water, a few grown-ups bobbed up and down with the waves.

"This is it?" I thought. Where were the kids my age? I wasn't going to just sit out there by myself and dig holes. And since swimming was off the table, thanks to my mom, there wasn't much left to do. Returning to the house being my only other option, I decided to just hang out on top of the dunes and watch for a while.

I took a seat in the sand, crossed my legs, and breathed in my surroundings. The sun felt hot on my face, but the breeze coming off the water made it tolerable. And it seemed quiet, kind of like the porch. Apart from the waves, most of the noise came from a little hole-digging kid straight in front of me, about halfway to the water. He'd been whining loudly about something to his mother. Not too long removed from this style of parental manipulation, I appreciated what he was trying to do, or at least how he was going about it.

Doing her best to ignore him, the mom sat in a fold-out beach chair just a few feet away. Beer in hand, she'd been trying to have a conversation with a woman in the chair next to her. Apparently, she hadn't learned that most kid tantrums can far outlast most moms' ability to ignore them. When she'd finally had enough, she stood up, towered over him, and – yelling, mind you – told him to stop crying and have fun. "You're at the beach!" was her closing argument.

The crying stopped as the boy watched his mother. When she plopped back down in her chair, the rear legs folded underneath sending her backward, her feet flying over her head, and her beer splashing all over her face. I don't know who laughed harder, me or the little kid. Regardless, he did stop whining.

"Get off the dunes!" I heard a man shout behind me.

I turned to my right to see an old man, about my uncle's age, standing on the deck of his beachfront house glaring at me. He repeated his demand, waving his arms in the air. "You're not supposed to be on those!" he added. "Get off!"

A little confused as to what I had done wrong, I looked at him and raised my hands with a shrug, body language for *I have no idea why you're yelling at me*. He didn't like that.

"Don't make me come out there!" he threatened, pointing his finger.

That was enough for me. I jumped up, slid down the backside of the dunes, and headed back toward the street. Of course, I had to stop a couple of times to pull the little sticker balls from my feet. Each time, I glanced back to see if he was watching me. He was. Maybe he'd forgot to tell me to have fun while he was yelling at me. I was at the beach, after all.

Back at the house, I climbed the stairs quickly, knowing sweet consolation for my disappointing beach experience waited in the form of chocolate chip cookies. My aunt Sarah was in the kitchen stirring something in a big pot on the stove. It smelled like fish.

"How was the beach?" she asked.

I picked up a cookie from the plate on the counter and jumped right to the main event. "I got yelled at," I said, taking a bite.

She stopped stirring and looked at me. "Yelled at? By who?"

"Some man outside one of those houses that sit behind the sand dunes."

She turned her attention back to the pot and started stirring again. "Was he tall, thin, and have a crew cut?"

I chewed my cookie, which was very good by the way, and matched her description with my memory. "Yes, ma'am. That was him."

She put the lid on the pot and rinsed her spoon in the sink. "And were you standing on the sand dunes when he yelled at you?"

"I was sitting on them," I said, holding my cookie in ready position. "How did you know?"

"That was Frank Wilson, honey," she said, turning around to open the refrigerator. "I've never met him, but I heard he doesn't like people getting on the dunes near his house."

"Why not?" I asked. "It's just sand."

She poured what seemed a random amount of milk into whatever she was cooking and began stirring again. "The dunes are the only thing between his house and the ocean," she said. "He's afraid if people get on them, they'll get flattened down and they won't be there anymore. And then his house might get washed away."

I started another cookie and gave the man's concern a run through my mind. It didn't make sense. "But if he doesn't want his house to get washed away," I began, "why does he live so close to the ocean?"

"That's a good question, honey," she said, chuckling. "You just stay away from Mr. Wilson, OK? Will you do that for me?"

"Yes, ma'am," I said, though it seemed like an unnecessary request. I certainly didn't want to get yelled at again.

"Ran, honey, why don't you move your things from the den into your room? It's right here." She pointed behind her to a doorway next to the refrigerator.

I retrieved my pillowcase and duffle bag from where I had dropped them earlier and carried them to the bedroom. Except for a bed and nightstand, the room was empty. The bare walls, like the rest of the walls, floor, and ceiling in the house, were dark-stained wood panels. "Not very patriotic," I thought, missing my room at home. To the left of the bed was a bathroom about the size of my mom's closet. Tossing my bags on the bed, I plopped down next to them. The rusting blades of a white metal ceiling fan squeaked in slow circles above my head. So, this was home for a while, I thought.

I spent the rest of the day reading *Where the Red Fern Grows,* a testament to how little there was to do. I have to say, though, after I got past my irritation with the first chapter (Who lets a lost dog get lost again, on purpose?), I actually started to enjoy reading it. At least the story has dogs in it. They'd better not die in the end; that's all I cared about.

The big pot Aunt Sarah had been stirring earlier in the day turned out to be fish chowder, which she served with buttered toast for supper. At least I could look forward to eating while I was there. It didn't make up for the complete lack of everything else, but it helped.

After supper, I read on the porch until it got too dark. Aunt Sarah didn't like to turn on the porch light because it attracted bugs, she said. She joined me after she finished cleaning up the kitchen. When the porch got too dark, I retired to my room and read a bit more before turning off the light. I have no idea what time that was, but I never saw Uncle Breland.

FIVE

Sunday Morning Coming Down

For the second morning in a row, I found myself awake just before the sun came up. I'd spent half the night wrestling with my pillow to keep it from squishing between my bed's metal headboard rails. And the other half imagining my head getting stuck between them and the fire department having to cut me out with a chainsaw. Now, with the early morning light slowly making its way through the two uncovered windows behind my head, I lay there under the ceiling fan staring at the wood-paneled ceiling trying to get my bearings: I was really at the beach, alone with no dog, no friends, no air conditioning, no Captain Crunch cereal with Crunch Berries, and no TV. Did I mention no TV?

My eyes began to fill as I wondered what I'd done to deserve this three-month sentence of solitary confinement. Or two and a half, whatever. Maybe if I had made my bed more, or picked up my clothes, or even offered to cut the grass once in a while, I would've woken up in my own bed instead of this creaky, lumpy, spring-loaded, sheet-covered, sweat sponge. But, in all honesty, I didn't like cleaning my room or doing laundry, and I hated yardwork. So, there I was, alone at the beach.

I rolled onto my stomach and propped a pillow under my chest so I could look out the window. The sun hadn't risen above the row of houses fronting the beach yet, but the sky above them was bright orange, fading to blue. As my gaze dropped from the empty sky to the shadows thrown across the road before our house, I saw a barefoot girl in shorts and a t-shirt walking down the street. I grabbed the headboard rails and pulled myself closer to the window. My eyes dried quickly, and my heart began to beat a little faster. She looked about my age. A sudden rush of hope flushed through my body. It was like I had landed on the barren, desolation of the moon only to look out my lunar module window and see a cute girl casually strolling across the Sea of Tranquility. There was life on the beach. But who was she? What was her name? Were there more like her? Why was she walking down the street so early in the morning? Is that a thing kids do here? My pondering of those important, potentially summer-altering questions was suddenly interrupted by a heavy-handed knock on my door.

"Time to get up, kid," I heard my uncle Breland say.

I rolled over and stared at the door without answering. I considered making loud snoring sounds, but I wasn't quick enough. The door opened slowly as he peered into my room without entering. I took a quick glance back out the window, but the girl was gone.

"Time to get up," he repeated from the doorway.

Uncle Breland was a few inches taller than my dad. And about eight years older. That summer, he would have been getting close to fifty. But at the time, he seemed so much older to me. His dark hair was beginning to gray. His face looked worn and stubbly, except for his thick Burt Reynolds mustache. The dark circles under his eyes completed his brooding old-man look. Toss in a smoldering cigarette hanging out of his mouth and you get the picture.

"Morning, Uncle Breland," I offered as I sat up. He didn't answer right away. I watched his eyes travel around the room slowly as if he were looking for something. "Are we going somewhere?" I asked.

"*We're* not going anywhere," he answered, seeming a bit grumpy. "You are."

My immediate thought? I was going home! Maybe my mom felt bad and was coming back to get me. Or maybe my friends held a mass protest outside our house like all those anti-war hippies! "Where am I going?" I asked, hopefully.

"You've got work to do," he said, plainly without making eye contact.

"Work?" I repeated back to him. "You mean like a job?"

This time he did lock eyes with mine. "If you're gonna live here, you've got to earn your keep."

"But my mom didn't say anything about a job," I assured him.

"Well, your mom's not here, is she?" he said, a little irritation in his voice. "She dumped you on the beach like a sea turtle and took off. Now get up, and put some clothes on." He turned and walked away.

"But what am I going to do?" I called out from my bed.

"Get up, Turtle," he answered from the den.

Great. I'd seen Uncle Breland for all of thirty seconds and he'd already tagged me with a nickname. Maybe it was just a one-time thing, I hoped.

He reappeared in the doorway. "And you'd better eat something, Turtle," he added. "You've got a long day ahead of you."

Turtle. I guess that was better than Oompa-Loompa. But whatever he had in mind for me sounded worse than being locked in a closet. Fortunately, Aunt Sarah appeared in my doorway a moment later, tying an apron around her waist.

"Are you hungry?" she asked.

"Yes, ma'am," I answered, thankfully.

She offered to make pancakes and bacon, which I eagerly accepted. At least that would delay whatever Uncle Breland had in mind for a half hour or so.

I had slept in my clothes so there was no need to get dressed. I swung my feet off the bed onto the sandy floor and joined Aunt Sarah in the kitchen. Uncle Breland sat in a rocking chair on the front porch smoking a cigarette, staring at the ocean.

I took a seat at the small white and chrome-plated kitchen table just outside my bedroom door. It sat flush against the wall with three yellow-cushioned chairs around it. Watching my aunt work in the kitchen was like watching Bob Griese run the Miami Dolphins' offense. She was a model of contented efficiency. As the smell of bacon began to fill the kitchen, I summoned the courage to ask what kind of work my uncle had in store for me.

"Hey, Aunt Sarah?"

"Yes, honey?" she answered, undistracted from her pancake batter mixing.

"Do you know what Uncle Breland wants me to do this morning?"

"Oh, nothing to worry about," she said, pouring batter onto the hot griddle. "Just some yardwork."

"Yardwork?" I repeated, with added emphasis. I began to sense a conspiracy. Did my dad tell Uncle Breland how much I hated yardwork? Was this all part of some elaborate scheme to punish me for not cutting the grass? And more importantly, did Uncle Breland break his own TV antenna to keep me from watching *American Bandstand*?

"I have to go to church," my aunt said, pulling me out of my rabbit hole. "But I'll be back to make you lunch."

As I sat at the table brooding, she served my breakfast waitress-style, complete with syrup, extra napkins, and an offer to get me some more butter. But something about the yardwork was not making sense. Then it occurred to me. "Aunt Sarah," I said, "this house doesn't have a yard."

"It's not for here, Turtle," said Uncle Breland, appearing in the kitchen. "When you finish eating, I'll be on the porch."

SIX

Why Me

As I ate the pancakes Aunt Sarah made for my breakfast, I decided she was definitely not part of the conspiracy to ruin my summer. Like yesterday's PB&J, chocolate chip cookies, and fish chowder, the pancakes were worthy of some sort of award given to women who cook really good food for their nephews. I tried to eat them slowly to delay my yardwork with Uncle Breland, but I couldn't. Fluffy, crispy, buttery, and as big around as my plate, they were gone before Aunt Sarah had even left the kitchen.

"Have you had a sufficiency?" she asked me, wiping down the green countertop.

I crunched the last of my bacon and thought about how to answer that. I had never heard "sufficiency" used in a sentence before, much less one directed at me. But context clues gave me enough to offer up an answer. "I'm stuffed. Thank you, ma'am."

She untied her apron, hung it on the hook next to the pantry door, and stepped over to their black rotary desk phone sitting on a small round table just inside the den. As I watched her patiently go through the repetitive circular motion of dialing a number, I wondered if she was calling my mom to tell her how much I ate for breakfast. Holding the receiver to her ear, all she said was, "Hey, I'm ready," and hung up.

Definitely not my mom.

She turned back to me with a smile. "I'll see you after church," she said.

She disappeared into their bedroom for a second, came out with shoes on her feet and a Bible in her hands, and stepped out onto the porch. I watched her say something to my uncle, who seemed to ignore her, then head out the screen door and down the steps. I was officially alone in the house with Uncle Breland. Which, coincidentally, gave me a sudden concern for my oral hygiene. I left the kitchen quickly for the safety of my bathroom and closed the door.

After loading my toothbrush with Crest, I extended my usual ten-second brushing routine into an open-ended workout. I needed more stalling tactics. Or was there something I could say or do that would get me out of the yardwork, altogether? I appealed to my reflection in the small mirror over the sink for ideas. I could say I was allergic to grass! My eyes brightened for a moment until I imagined what my uncle would likely say: "Not my problem, Turtle."

As the white ring of foam around my mouth grew larger and larger, I realized I had no other ideas. And my arm was getting tired. I spit, rinsed, and gave up.

I made my way out onto the porch and found my uncle rocking slowly in his chair. "Hey, Uncle Breland," I said, "I'm ready."

He turned his head without disrupting his rocking and gave me the once-over. "Where are your shoes?" he asked looking at my flip-flops.

"On my feet," I replied.

He shook his head, got up slowly from his chair, and walked past me toward the screen door. Assuming I was supposed to follow, I walked down the stairs behind him. Once on the ground, he pointed underneath the stair landing. "Grab what's behind that bike under there," he said.

I moved around Uncle Breland to get a better look. An old red and white Schwinn Flying Star bicycle sat in the darkness beneath the stairs. Its tires were flat. Its chain and white fenders were rusty. But, with its aerodynamic fake gas tank, painted carrying rack behind the seat, and chrome handlebars, it still looked pretty nifty to me. "Does that bike work?" I asked.

"Don't worry about the bike," said my uncle. "Get the mower and hedge clippers from under there. You should see a rake too."

I moved the bike and grabbed the handle of what I assumed to be the lawn mower. Its long handle stretched down to two small wheels connected by three spiral metal blades. There was no motor. "Oh, no," I may have said out loud. I'd heard about these. My friend Danny Kelly's grandfather made him cut his yard with one once. He said he had to push the mower over the whole yard three times to get all the grass cut. He still talked about it eight months later.

I pulled the mower out and ducked under the landing for the rest of it.

"Hand me the rake and trimmers and follow me," my uncle said. "And keep that mower out of the sand."

Without saying anything else, he began walking north, with me pushing the mower on the street behind him. The early morning air felt good. The sun had crept over the beachfront houses, but it wasn't hot, despite the lack of a breeze. I hadn't seen anyone outside yet, my mystery girl being the exception. About two blocks up, we turned left on a little cut-through street that connected the beach road to the creek road. We crossed to the other side of the creek road and continued north.

The houses along the way seemed smaller and older than those closer to the beach. I guess to compensate for facing the creek instead of the ocean, each house had a long, wooden walkway stretching through the high marsh grass to where the water ran wider. Most of the boardwalks ended with a small, covered pavilion. I made a mental note to walk out to the end of one of those before the summer was over.

"That's it right there," my uncle said, pointing ahead to the ugliest thing I'd seen on the island.

Before us, off the left side of the road, was a small mobile home trailer. Backed up all the way to the high marsh grass, it looked abandoned. Two large bushes grew on either side of the three wooden steps leading up to its only door. Around, behind, and underneath grew tall grass and weeds. Several strands of ivy had grown up the side of the trailer around the side window.

We left the street and stood on the sand and gravel surrounding the trailer.

"Who lives here?" I asked.

"That's not your concern," he said, looking at the trailer. "See those bushes? I want you to cut those back to about…" He paused and turned his eyes to me. Bumping the middle of my chest with a light karate chop, he said, "Right here. Got it?"

"Yes, sir," I answered.

"And all that stuff growing underneath and up the side there, I want that gone."

"What do I do with it? The stuff I cut, I mean."

"Just make a pile near the marsh grass behind the trailer." He laid the hedge clippers and rake on the ground before me. "Get to work, Turtle," he said, turning to walk away.

"How long am I supposed to do all this?" I asked.

"As long as it takes," he said without looking back. "You've got all summer."

SEVEN

Lean On Me

Uncle Breland had been gone a few minutes. He had walked up the creek road, took the turn toward the beach, and was out of sight. I could breathe a sigh of relief about that, but I hadn't moved an inch since he left. I stood there looking at the wild mess in front of me. *Why does this matter?* I wondered. Even if I did clean it up, it was still just an old mobile home sitting on a trailer with a ridiculous light green racing stripe down its side. As if the stripe made you forget it's a one-room shack on wheels. And what if the person who lived there came back while I was working? What would I say? Part of me wanted to run and hide somewhere. I briefly imagined life as a yardwork fugitive trapped on Pawleys Island. But then I would miss out on all of Aunt Sarah's good cooking. I sighed, picked up the rusty hedge clippers, and stepped toward the trailer.

I climbed the three steps to the front door to get a better angle at the overgrown bushes. Opening the giant scissors, I maneuvered a branch between the blades and squeezed. Nothing happened. I tried again, even harder, and got the same result. Already frustrated with my lack of yard skills, I took a seat on the top step and reconsidered life as a fugitive.

Intruding on my vacant stare down the creek road was a boy carrying a small cooler. Although still a good distance away, he seemed a few inches shorter than me but carried himself like someone older than he looked. As he continued along in my direction, I tried to think of plausible explanations for why I was sitting on the stairs of this nasty trailer. I thought about just being honest: *My grumpy old uncle hates me so much he's making me do yardwork for strangers.* But who would believe that? How about: *My girlfriend lives here. I'm just waiting for her to wake up.* That sounded worse than the truth. Before I could come up with anything else, he was passing right in front of me.

He looked my way, nodded his head upward, and said, "Hey, what's up?"

"I don't live here," I heard myself say.

He came to a stop. "What?"

"I mean, this isn't my house," I explained, pointing my thumb over my shoulder. "I'm just doing yardwork."

"Oh, far out," he said casually. "What's your name?"

"I'm Ran," I said. "What's yours?"

"Joey. I live over there, across the creek." He pointed to the mainland side of the marsh. "You're not from here, are you?"

"No, I'm from Columbia. I'm just here for the summer."

His eyes bounced around my overgrown surroundings. "So, you're just trying to earn some bread?"

"No, my uncle's making me," I said.

"He lives here?"

"No. He lives over there," I said pointing toward the house.

"So, who lives here?"

I shrugged my shoulders. "I don't know."

My new friend looked confused. "All right, well…" he said, beginning to move on.

"What's in the cooler?" I asked, forcing conversation. Any time spent talking was time not doing yardwork.

"Oh, nothing yet," Joey said. "I'm heading down to the creek to check a crab trap. Wanna come?"

"I don't know," I said, wanting to say yes. "I'm supposed to be cutting these bushes."

He laughed. "You don't look like you want to be doing that."

"I don't," I said, glancing up at the branch I failed to cut. "I'm not even sure how."

He looked down the street for a moment, then back at me. "OK, well," he began, "how about you help me with the crabs now, and then I help you with the bushes after. Deal?"

Negotiating with another kid was so much easier than with grown-ups. "Deal," I said, jumping off the stairs. I pushed the mower, rake, and clippers under the trailer and joined Joey on the street.

"How old are you?" he asked, as we started walking.

"I'm going into seventh grade," I said. "I'm twelve. Almost thirteen. How about you?"

"Same," said Joey.

"Do you have a girlfriend?" I asked.

"No," he said. "Why, do you?"

"No," I admitted. "Are there a lot of girls our age around here?"

"Some, yeah," he said. "I guess."

"I haven't seen any since I got down here."

"When did you get here?"

"Yesterday," I said.

He laughed. "You're in a hurry, aren't you?"

I didn't really have an answer for that, so I let it go. "I did see this girl walking down the street past our house super early this morning."

After a few steps, he asked, "Did she have long brown hair?"

I thought for a moment. "It wasn't that light out, yet, but I think so."

"It was probably this girl named Joni," he said.

I had a slight déjà vu from my conversation with Aunt Sarah about Mr. Wilson the day before. "Does everybody know everybody around here?" I asked.

"I guess. It's just that Joni likes to go on the beach and watch the sun come up. So, it was probably her. Kind of weird if you ask me. For a kid, I mean. Come on, it's up here on the left."

"What is?" I asked, trying to keep up.

"The crab trap," he said, quickening his pace. "Follow me."

At the end of the street beside a creek boat ramp sat a three-story white house with dark green trim. I followed Joey around to the back of the house where all three levels had screened porches overlooking the marsh. He seemed to be in sneaking mode, so I followed quietly. But I stopped when, without hesitation, he climbed over the wood railing of a boardwalk extending from the back porch to the creek, maneuvering right past a sign that said "Private." I looked around to see if anyone was watching. I suddenly realized I didn't know Joey at all. He could've been one of those kids who steal your lunch money to buy firecrackers to throw at squirrels. Please excuse the Donaldson twin reference, but the point is I didn't know Joey. And here I was tagging along with him. And getting arrested my first full day at the beach was not what I had in mind when I woke up.

Joey turned and waved me on.

"Do you know these people," I asked in a loud whisper, pointing toward the house. It was still early, and I was afraid of waking someone.

"No, but my dad does," he said. "They're totally down with it. Come on."

I quickly weighed the thought of getting arrested against spending the rest of the day doing yardwork. That was all it took. I put my hands on top of the boardwalk railing and climbed over. I trotted a few steps to catch up and walked with Joey to the end of the boardwalk and under the covered deck. I checked that off my to-do list a lot earlier than I expected.

Joey pulled some work gloves from his back pockets and handed them to me. "Here, put these on," he said.

"Why?" I asked, sliding my hands into the leather gloves.

"You're gonna get the crabs for me," said Joey. He pointed to a rope tied around one of the deck's corner posts. "Just kneel down here and pull this rope up."

"What am I pulling up?" I asked, still feeling cautious.

"Hopefully a bunch of crabs," he said.

I knelt on the deck, reached under the bottom railing, and grabbed hold of the rope. "Got it," I said.

"Now, just pull it up."

I settled back on my knees and began pulling, hand over hand. Joey leaned over the top railing and watched my progress.

After a few more tugs upward, I heard the splashing sound of something emerging from the water. I looked down to see a wire mesh cube about two feet wide on all sides dangling from the rope. Inside, a lone blue crab clung to a mesh cone in the center. Joey reached over the rail, grabbed the trap, and pulled it onto the deck. He looked disappointed.

"You got a crab," I said for lack of anything else to say. "What do you do with them?"

"We eat 'em," he said, lifting the trap up to eye level. He studied the crab as it clung tightly to the cone. "My dad likes to make crab soup. It's so stellar. But we need more than one crab."

"What's inside that thing he's holding onto?"

"It's a chicken neck. That's what you use for bait."

"Crabs eat chicken?" I asked.

"That and other crabs," he said, his eyes focused on the crab. "Take off the gloves."

I pulled the wet gloves off my hands. "Now what?" I asked.

"I want you to reach in there and pull him out for me. We're gonna set him free."

"What? No way," I said, recoiling. "I'm not gonna get pinched."

"It's easy," said Joey. "Look, I'll show you."

Joey reached into the trap and showed me how to pick up the crab. I found it a little unsettling to be taking instruction from another twelve-year-old. But he seemed to possess unusual self-confidence for his age.

"Now you try," he said, stepping back.

I reached in and moved my hand behind the crab, just like Joey showed me. I placed my thumb on the center of its smooth shell and my fingers underneath its body.

"Just don't squeeze it," Joey said.

As I lifted the crab from the trap, its legs swam in all directions while its alien-looking eyes searched for a way to pinch my fingers. "What do I do with it now?" I asked, holding it at arm's length.

"Just lower it down to the water and drop it. They break easy so don't throw it or anything."

I knelt back down on the wooden deck, stretched my arm under the railing, and lowered the crab as far as I could before dropping it into the water. For some reason, I was sad to see it disappear into the green current below.

"Oh well," said Joey, tossing the trap back into the water. He reached down for his cooler. "Let's go knock out those bushes."

I knew that was our deal, but his offer still surprised me. "You're really gonna help me do that?" I asked, as we began our walk back on the boardwalk. "But you didn't get any crabs."

"You helped me; I'll help you," he said with a shrug. "That was our deal."

As I was thinking how nice it felt to have a new friend I could trust, the sound of a door closing came from the house at the end of the boardwalk.

"Uh-oh," said Joey, looking up at the porch. "Come on." He lowered himself and began moving quickly with quiet strides to where we had climbed over the railing.

Though a little confused about what was happening, I followed Joey's lead. We leapt over the railing onto the pavement and hurried around the side of the house back to the creek road. Once past the house, I jogged a few steps to catch up.

"What just happened?" I asked, now walking in stride with Joey.

"We almost got caught," he said, plainly.

"Caught? You said it was OK for us to be out there."

"Yeah, well, I kinda lied about that," he said.

"You what? You lied?"

"Sure," he said, "but don't get all freaked out about it. Nothing happened."

"We could've been arrested," I said, going back to my original fear.

He laughed. "We didn't do anything. Just chill."

I walked beside him for a moment, trying to reconstruct the last ten minutes in light of Joey's confession. "So, was that your crab trap?" I asked.

"No."

His sudden honesty about his dishonesty was a bit morally confusing. "Whose was it?"

"The people who live there."

"And you were going to steal their crabs?"

"No, you were," he said, laughing.

It was hard for me not to appreciate the humor in that, but I pressed on with my cross-examination. "That's why you had me put on the gloves and pull up the rope and take the crab out?"

"You catch on quick," he said, still smiling. "Look, you just got here; you didn't know any better. It was going to be an easy excuse if we got caught."

What twelve-year-old thinks like that? I wondered. "So, does your dad really know the people who live there?"

"He does."

Still trying to understand, I asked the obvious question. "So then, why would you want to steal their crabs?"

"That's between me and them," he said, his attention now fixed firmly ahead. "Come on, let's get your yardwork done."

Before us on the right side of the road sat the trailer, its ugliness basking in the morning sun. Since leaving it twenty minutes earlier, I'd made a new friend, trespassed on private property, attempted theft of fresh seafood, obtained new crabbing skills, and suffered the betrayal of a friend. I had returned older. And wiser.

EIGHT

Make Me Smile

Just a couple of months before I was sent to the beach, my friend, Pete Abel, invited me to a spring break party at his house. We swam in his pool all day and, after his dad grilled hot dogs for our supper, his mom took us to see the new *Charlotte's Web* movie. Though the title character was a spider who could spell, the movie was really about a little pig named Wilbur. Wilbur was an unwanted pig, sold off to the owner's brother who only wanted to see him get slaughtered. See where I'm going with this? But a new friend (spoiler alert) helps Wilbur triumph over the uncle and live a long and happy life wallowing in mud and playing with spiders.

I didn't like rolling in mud or playing with spiders, but after the work was done at the trailer, I felt a little like Wilber. Despite my uncle's intention to see me suffer through several days of sweat and frustration, the job was done before lunch, thanks to my new friend Joey. He did most of the hard stuff, cutting all the bushes and pulling off the ivy. I took care of the grass and weeds, pushing my uncle's stone-age mower around and around and around and under the trailer. Danny Kelly wasn't kidding about those things.

After we finished, Joey simply picked up his cooler, said "Later days," and walked away down the street. He had helped me defeat my uncle's plan to make me miserable. And while I was thankful, I wasn't sure what to make of Joey. When we met, he seemed like a good kid. Then he didn't. Then he did. But whatever or whoever he was, he was the only person under forty I knew on the island.

After Joey left, I loaded the rake and hedge clippers on the mower and pushed it back to the house. I moved the bike, rolled everything under the staircase landing, then headed up to the porch.

Uncle Breland sat alone, smoking. He didn't seem happy to see me. Rocking slowly in his creaky porch chair, he took the cigarette out of his mouth and asked, "What are you doing back here so soon?"

"I'm all done," I said, trying to pass through the porch quickly.

"All done, huh?" he said, watching me through the cloud of smoke hovering around his head.

I stopped before entering the den and turned to face him. "Yes, sir," I said, beginning to feel a little nervous. What other forms of torture did he have in mind for me? I looked around for help from my aunt but didn't see her. "Is Aunt Sarah home, yet?" I asked, hoping to steer the discussion toward food.

Uncle Breland ignored my question and lifted himself from his rocking chair. "Come with me," he said.

He led me back down the stairs to the street and went left just as we did earlier that morning. I assumed he was taking me back to the trailer for some reason, but since my uncle wasn't much for small talk, I didn't ask. I just walked behind him quietly wondering if his leathery bare feet could feel all the bumps from the small stones in the pavement. And if those round sticker things just crushed harmlessly beneath him.

After we arrived at the trailer, he stood motionless, his hands on his hips as he surveyed our work. He looked down at me. "You did all this?" he asked.

Afraid that including Joey would complicate things, I just said, "Yes, sir."

He looked back at the trailer, then back at me. "All by yourself. No one helped you."

"Um…yes, sir," I lied.

"Careful, Turtle. I'll ask you again, did anyone help you?"

Either I wasn't as good a liar as Joey, or his excellent bush-trimming skills gave me away. "Yes, sir," I confessed.

"Who?"

"I made a new friend, and he helped me."

"A new friend, huh? Did you promise him anything for helping you?"

"No, sir."

He looked at the trailer for a long moment and said, "Next time I give you something to do, it's for you to do. Not anyone else." Turning his head to me, he added, "Understand?"

No, I really didn't understand. What difference did it make if someone helped me? But I was afraid to ask that. "Yes, sir," I said.

"Good," he said, sternly.

With that, we walked back to the house the same way we came, with me following behind in my uncle's footsteps. As we rounded the corner back onto our street, he stopped quickly, shouted, "Ouch!" and began hopping on one foot. He turned and laid his heavy hand on my shoulder for balance while he pulled a round sticker thing from the arch of his other foot. In some weird way, I was happy to see it happen to him, just like it happened to me.

"Damn sandspurs," he said, tossing it into the street before continuing toward the house.

"Is that what you call them?" I asked, hurrying up a bit to walk along beside him.

"Why, what do you call them?" he answered.

"I just call 'em round sticker things."

He glanced down at me. "I guess that works too," he said. I thought I saw the slightest, almost imperceptible smile hiding underneath his dark mustache, if only for a second. Then it was gone.

We walked ahead to the house side by side, him on the pavement and me on the sand. We didn't say anything else. I knew it wasn't much, but that was the first real conversation I'd ever had with Uncle Breland. Just the two of us guys, walking down the street talking about round sticker things, or sandspurs. I suddenly felt lighter as we headed up the stairs of the house. Aunt Sarah was there waiting on the porch.

"You boys hungry?" she asked.

I had survived my first twenty-four hours at the beach.

NINE

Puppy Love

The following week settled into a steady, predictable routine of quiet boredom. Ironically, my school-assigned summer reading had become my primary source of entertainment. While the book was good, I was a little surprised by all the animal fighting in it. Dogs fighting dogs, dogs fighting raccoons, raccoons fighting people, people whacking raccoons on the head with clubs. As I read, I sometimes wondered what I was supposed to be learning from it all. Was there going to be a test on how to tree a raccoon at the end of the summer? If so, I'd be ready.

For most of the week, Uncle Breland was nowhere to be found. He was always gone when I woke up. Fishing, I assumed. When he was there, all he did was eat or sit in his porch rocking chair smoking cigarettes. Aunt Sarah cooked and cleaned, and came and went, usually to the grocery store. On Thursday morning, she took me with her to Marlow's Super Market, just across the marsh on the highway heading back toward Georgetown. A brick building about the size of my parent's house, it had an ice bin out front and a single gas pump. Inside were rows of shelves stocked with all the essentials and a butcher shop in the back. As we strolled the aisles, my aunt read from her shopping list and told me what to pull off the shelves. As a reward for loading our cart, she pointed me toward a big glass jar full of Lance cookies sitting on the checkout counter.

"Why don't you grab something for yourself, Ran," she said. "You can have three."

I lifted the jar's red metal lid, reached in, and pulled out three packs of Nekots, my favorites. She also sprung for a cold bottle of Pepsi, a must when you're eating Nekots.

65

"Rad choice, dude," I heard a familiar voice say behind me.

I turned around to see Joey. I quickly tried to think of an equally cool way to say hello, but since he already used *rad* and *dude*, my brain scrolled past *hey brotha, youngblood,* or *man*, before I just said, "Hey, Joey."

"How's it going?" he asked, moving to the end of the counter.

"Good. You know, just chillin' at the house," I said, sounding slightly more with it. I introduced Joey to my aunt Sarah and learned that he worked as a bag boy at the store.

"Hey, what are you doing later?" he asked, as he bagged our groceries. "I get off work at noon; you wanna hit the beach?"

"Sure, that sounds great," I said, glancing up at Aunt Sarah. She gave me a nod of approval.

"Just meet me at the pier at about one o'clock," said Joey.

I now had something to look forward to, but Aunt Sarah had one more errand to run and, unfortunately, she took me with her. She drove us to Litchfield, just north of Pawleys to a beauty parlor. My worst fear was being trapped there for two hours while she sat under one of those big, plastic, half-moon hair dryer things like my mom did sometimes. But thankfully, she wasn't there to get her hair done; she just needed to talk with someone who worked there. I sat down next to the front desk and waited. Aunt Sarah talked with one of the hairdresser ladies who was putting pieces of tinfoil in a woman's hair. Three other women sat underneath the hair dryers reading magazines. Whenever I looked in their direction, they would cut their eyes at me without moving their heads and smile like I was a puppy or something. After a few minutes, Aunt Sarah called me back to where she was.

"Ran, this is Ms. Mary," she said, introducing me to the hairdresser.

"Hi," I said, unsure of what was happening.

"Hello, Ran," she said offering her hand. "Thank you for taking care of my yard. It looks so much better."

"Ms. Mary lives in the trailer you worked on Sunday," my aunt added, unnecessarily.

"Oh, you're welcome," I said, letting go of Ms. Mary's hand.

"I'll call you later, Mary," said my aunt, as she turned my shoulders toward the exit.

"She's a nice lady," Aunt Sarah said, as we left the salon.

"Uh-huh," I said, wondering again why I had been tasked with cleaning the hair lady's yard. I shook the thought from my head as we got in Aunt Sarah's car and set my mind on the beach.

After lunch on the porch, which consisted of another crunchy PB&J and four Nekot cookies, I headed out to meet Joey. To avoid getting yelled at by Mr. Wilson, I walked down the street to a public access pathway and made my way onto the beach. The tide was about halfway up, but I couldn't tell if it was going out or coming in. With just a slight breeze drifting over the sand, the ocean was smooth. Small waves rolled in clean and orderly, washing over my feet as I walked along the shoreline. Up ahead, just past the pier, a small crowd of girls stood facing the water. With a quick look through the pier pilings, I could see what held their interest. A group of surfer boys sat on their boards just behind the waves. I stopped and watched from a distance.

The boys seemed to be taking turns pointing their boards toward shore. They'd paddle along with a swell and stand up as the wave curled beside them. Some would do little turns, but most just stood there. Each ride only lasted a few seconds, but the girls watching would clap and cheer every time. It seemed like a lot of excitement over nothing. Maybe their TV antennas were broken too, I thought.

As I watched the surfers and the girls watching them, Joey called to me from the steps of a boardwalk extending over the dunes on my side of the pier. I gave him a wave, and he started toward me leading a small beagle on a leash. I immediately wished I had pressed my mom harder about letting Pepper stay. That could be me, I thought.

"Hey, man," said Joey, the dog pulling him toward me to say hello.

"Is that your dog?" I asked. I got down on my knees and rubbed the dog's black, brown, and white back as it wiggled with excitement.

"No, it's our neighbor's," he said. "I borrowed him today just for you."

I couldn't tell if he was joking. "What do you mean?"

"You want to meet girls, don't you?"

"I guess, but what does that have to do with the dog?"

Joey laughed. "Trust me, dude. On the beach, dogs are like girl magnets."

I stood up, brushed the sand off my knees, and pointed toward the pier. "Speaking of girls," I said, "there's a whole bunch right over there."

"Why do you think I told you to meet me at the pier?" he asked, as we began walking in their direction. "Whenever the surfer dudes are out, so are the girls. Here, take the dog."

I took the leash from Joey and watched the dog follow his nose along the sand as he trotted beside me.

"If they ask, he's your dog," said Joey. "Just play along."

"OK," I said. I was more than happy with that arrangement. I knew nothing about surfing and even less about girls, but I knew dogs.

As we walked closer, I couldn't help but survey the girls in front of us. With all of them facing the ocean, they were unaware or uninterested in our approach. "Most of these girls look a lot older than we do," I said, a little concerned.

"Don't worry about it," said Joey as we passed under the pier. "Come on. I see a girl I know; you might like her."

I suddenly didn't care who Joey knew. My eyes had already filtered out every girl but one. She was tanned, leggy, blonde, and wore a white bikini. I was looking at the most beautiful girl I'd ever seen. (In person, that is. If Olivia Newton-John had been standing there watching the boys surf, I would have given that prize to her. But since Olivia wasn't available...)

"Which one?" I asked to be polite.

"The one in the white bikini," said Joey.

"*That* girl?" I asked, unaware that I was pointing. "You know *that* girl?"

"Yeah, she goes to my school," said Joey, pulling down my pointing arm. "She's a year older than us, though."

"I'm down with that," I said, smiling.

Joey stopped and pulled me back a step. "Just let me do the talking, OK? She's not like other girls."

"What do you mean?"

"Just trust me."

Joey seemed to say that a lot. Maybe I should start keeping score on how often it worked out to my advantage. But once again, I went along with it. "Sure, OK."

I watched Joey stroll casually up to the white bikini girl a few steps ahead of me and my four-legged wingman.

"Hey, Heather," he said, pulling her attention away from the surfers.

"Hey," she said, quickly turning her gaze back to the ocean.

"What's up?" asked Joey.

"Surfs up, that's what's up," she said without looking at him.

"Far out," said Joey, still unable to draw her interest.

I was new to the whole "walk up to a girl on the beach and start talking" thing, but it didn't seem to be going well.

Joey gave me a quick glance and a reassuring nod before introducing me. "Hey, this is my friend, Ran."

She turned and looked directly at me with glistening blue eyes. The light breeze blew silky strands of golden hair lightly across her perfect face. I stood there like a mannequin, unable to move or speak. It was Olivia Newton-John all over again. My only hope for conversation with Heather rested in the cuteness of the beagle now licking himself on the sand next to me.

"Do you surf?" she asked me.

Before I could jumpstart my brain to answer, Joey inserted himself. "Not today," he said. "These little waves aren't worth us getting out there. We just came to dive off the end of the pier."

I felt my head spin in Joey's direction. What did he just say?

Heather cocked her head at Joey. "*You're* going to dive off the pier?" she asked, her eyes bouncing between the two of us. "I don't think you're allowed to do that."

"Well, you're not supposed to surf closer than a hundred feet from the pier either. But it's not stopping those dorks," said Joey pointing toward the surfers. He turned and motioned for me to follow. Taking the leash from my hand, he gave it to Heather. "Here, watch his dog for us."

Heather took the leash, looking slightly stunned. "What's his name?" she asked, as we walked away.

"Ran," I said, regaining my ability to speak.

"No, the dog," she said.

I had only said one word to Heather, and I still managed to look like an idiot.

"Ringo!" shouted Joey as we walked up the sand toward the pier entrance. "Like the Beatle!"

As I followed Joey up through the dunes and around to the pier entrance, we walked past a sign that said, "Condominium Residents Only, No Diving." For the second time in a week, Joey had me trespassing on private property. Lacking confidence in what we were about to do, I lagged a few steps behind his brisk pace while I thought about how to get out of it.

"Why did you tell her we're going to dive off the pier?" I asked for starters.

"Because we are," he said, striding confidently ahead on the pier's warm wooden planks.

I scurried up beside him. "But the sign said no diving."

"Don't worry about the sign."

"But we don't live in the condos either," I added.

"My dad knows people who live here. If anybody asks, just say we're guests of the Doars."

"Who are the Doars?"

"I don't know," Joey said with a shrug, "but everyone else seems to know who they are."

"But I'm not supposed to swim unless someone's watching me."

"Don't be a putz," he said. "Besides, Heather's watching you, isn't she?"

He had a point. But diving thirty feet into the ocean forty yards from shore? That was still up for debate.

As we neared the end of the pier, Joey stopped and turned me toward him. "Ok, here's how we do this," he said. "First, you don't look down at the water. If you look down before you dive, you won't do it."

I looked around us and back toward the pier entrance. I realized Joey had kept us in the center of the pier all the way out to the end. I hadn't had a chance to look over the railing and freak out about how high we were.

"Second thing," he continued, "and this is most important. Show me your hands."

I held out my hands, palms up. He turned them over.

"Now grab your right thumb with your left hand and make two fists. When you dive, keep your hands over your head just like this." He stretched his clenched fists far over his head. "Don't dive like Superman. Keep your fists together. You want them to hit the water first, not your head. Got it?"

I looked at my hands and squeezed my thumb as hard as possible. "Joey, I'm not sure about this," I said, shaking my head.

"OK. That's fine," he said, giving up surprisingly easy. "I'll do it, and you can just tell Heather you chickened out."

The image of Heather's face when she first looked at me ran through my mind. "What's next?" I asked, feeling a new sense of determination.

"OK," said Joey, back on task. "We're just gonna take a few steps back, I'll count to three, and then we go. Got it?"

"You've done this before?" I asked, hopefully.

"Sure, my dad and I do it all the time. And if you want a girl to like you, this beats surfing every time."

It was all happening so fast, the rational fear I should've felt was getting lost behind Joey's fast-paced instruction. I followed his lead as he backed up a few steps away from the railing.

"Ready?" Joey asked, spreading his feet apart like a runner at the start line.

I copied his stance, felt my heart racing in my chest, and said, "Ready."

Joey started counting. "One…"

What am I doing?! I thought to myself.

"Two…"

Oh my god! Oh my god!

"Three!"

Joey and I bolted toward the railing like two Olympic sprinters. I grabbed my thumb, flew up on the bench, and dove headfirst over the railing. I closed my eyes as I soared through the air and waited to hit the water below. And waited. Just when I was starting to wonder what was taking so long, my fists hit the water. The impact broke my grip on my thumb and jerked my left arm straight by my side as I surged downward. I kept my eyes closed, but I was still alive as far as I could tell.

I turned myself right-side up and swam to the surface. When my head emerged from the water, the sound of cheers from girls on the beach and surfer boys in the water filled my ears. I gave an embarrassed wave and looked around for Joey. He wasn't in the water, at least not where I could see him. But then I heard a hearty laugh and clapping from above.

"That was off the hook, dude!" Joey shouted from the pier, giving me two thumbs-up. "I'll meet you back on the beach!" With that, he disappeared from view.

I treaded water for a minute before swimming in, just floating alone next to the pier. I needed a moment to catch up with reality. Surprisingly, I wasn't mad at Joey. Yes, he totally faked me out, but I had just done something pretty amazing as a result. I began my swim to shore, crossing underneath the pier to avoid the surfers on my way in. I was able to body surf in a small wave before wading the rest of the way. Joey was waiting for me next to Heather and Ringo under the pier.

"That was awesome, dude!" he said as I approached.

"Did that hurt?" asked Heather, handing the leash back to me.

"No," I said. "It was pretty fun." I immediately wished I had said something less twelve-year-old-sounding, but it was already out there.

She smiled and said, "We're going to be at King's later if you want to come."

I froze again. First, I didn't know what or where King's was. And second, she was beautiful.

"We'll be there," Joey said, bailing me out again.

"Groovy," she said with a smile, before turning to rejoin her friends.

Joey hurried us away from under the pier and back up the beach. "Well?" he asked as we walked.

"Well?" I repeated back to him, unsure what he meant.

"Hello! You're welcome, dude!" he said, slapping my back. "I totally got you a date with Heather Altman!"

"Thank you," I said, sincerely. "But what is King's?"

TEN

Then Came You

I sat on the porch with Aunt Sarah while Joey took Ringo back to his neighbor so we could go to King's. I liked Ringo, but he didn't turn out to be the girl magnet that Joey had promised. Pepper, on the other hand, would've had girls standing in line all the way down the beach just waiting to talk to us. That would have been a lot easier than diving off a pier just to talk to one. But that one was Heather. And when she looked at me…that image of her face was now wall-papered inside my brain. But rather than just sitting in a rocking chair idly relating every thought back to Heather, I decided to read more of *Where the Red Fern Grows*.

My folded page corner was at the start of chapter eight. It was finally hunting season for young Billy, and he was obsessed with landing his first raccoon. So, he went off on his own, a young boy in the wilderness searching for what he thought would make him a man. OK, the book wasn't helping me get my mind off Heather.

I put the *Red Fern* down and started in on another pack of Nekots with a glass of Aunt Sarah's iced tea. I don't know why, but my aunt's tea tasted so much better than what my mom made at home. (No offense, Mom, if you're reading this.) I had seen her use the same Lipton tea bags we have at home, but when I asked about it, Aunt Sarah said the Georgetown County water was "different" from Columbia's.

"Does that have anything to do with how the air in Georgetown smells like poop?" I asked.

"I can't say," she said, staring ahead as she rocked slowly.

I didn't know if that meant it was a local secret or that she honestly didn't know. I decided to just drink my tea and enjoy the mystery.

I hadn't said anything to Aunt Sarah about diving off the pier. She would have had me on the phone with my mother in two seconds. But I did ask her about all the stuff Joey told me about King's. She said, simply, "Oh, I forgot to tell you about that." But here's how I heard it: "I forgot to tell you, Ran, my twelve-year-old nephew who sits around here with nothing to do, that there's a beach arcade with pinball machines, air hockey, foosball, trampolines, snow cones, and putt-putt golf right down the street from our house."

Obviously, I'd been too busy cutting grass, grocery shopping, and reading *Where the Red Fern Grows* to be bothered with little island details like King's Funland. It's no wonder I didn't see any kids my age on the beach the first time I went out there. They were probably all at King's. I guess when you're Aunt Sarah's age, fun isn't part of your daily thought process. But thanks to Heather Altman, by way of Joey, I was now in the know.

It was getting late in the afternoon, and I was growing tired of waiting for Joey. The whole Heather thing was making me nervous, and I didn't know why. Joey had said there was something different about her but didn't say what it was. I told Aunt Sarah I was going to venture down to King's by myself, but she suggested I wait until after we ate. Hmm…Heather Altman versus fried flounder and cheese grits. It took less than ten seconds for me to decide. Heather would just have to wait.

After supper, which included peach cobbler and ice cream for dessert, I searched through the clothes on my bedroom floor and found the money my mom had given me. I decided to take three one-dollar bills to King's. It seemed like a lot, but I didn't want to run out my first time there. As I passed through the porch, Aunt Sarah offered to send Joey to King's if he came looking for me. I thanked her and headed down the street.

About three blocks up on the right, nestled between the street and the dunes, sat the savior of my summer. King's

Funland. Near the street were four kids bouncing on trampolines inside a chain-link fence. The trampolines were the big rectangular kind, but instead of being stretched across a raised metal frame, they were ground level with big holes dug beneath them. Behind the trampolines was a small putt-putt golf course. No one was playing on it, but still, it was an option. The arcade building sat behind the putt-putt course. It was a plain, cream-colored, corrugated metal building stretching all the way to the dunes. It looked like a warehouse.

Turning right at the trampolines, I left the street and made my way up the sandy lane to the arcade. I bounced up the three wood-plank steps through the wide, open-air entrance and stopped. It was just how Joey described it. Kids rolled heavy wooden balls up Skee-ball lanes lining the wall to my left. The ringing bells of a half-dozen pinball machines being played across the arcade could be heard over a loud jukebox in the far corner. Air hockey and foosball tables occupied the green-painted concrete floor in between. On the beach side of the building, a large open overhead door let the salty ocean air drift over the dunes and through the arcade.

To my right, a snack counter boasting "snowballs" and hot buttered popcorn lined the back wall. A lone barstool sat in front of the order window. I decided to just take a seat and wait. As I approached, a girl about my age greeted me from behind the counter.

"Hey, what can I get for you?" she asked with a smile.

"Can I just sit here while I wait for my friend?" I asked, my eyes still scanning for Heather.

"Sure," the girl said. "What's your name? I'm Joni."

I wasn't expecting an introduction, so it took me a second to catch up. "Oh, I'm Ran," I said as I looked around the arcade.

"Ran," she repeated. "Hey, if you say our names together real fast it sounds like Italian food. Ranjoni!"

Grunt. I leaned a bit forward off the stool so I could see two girls outside the entrance, but they didn't come in. And neither one was Heather. Settling back on the stool, I realized the girl behind the counter had just asked me a question. "I'm sorry, what?" I asked.

"Are you here just for the week?" she asked.

"No, for the summer," I said, looking at the foosball table. I tried to imagine playing a game against Heather. But that might get a little confusing. I'd feel bad if I beat her and like a dork if I lost. While I was weighing that out in my head, I missed something else from the counter girl. "Sorry?" I asked.

"I said you'll probably be here a lot, then. You can try all our snowball flavors! They're really just snow cones, but we call them snowballs."

"Uh-huh," I said. Technically I was listening to her, but I was screening out things I really didn't need to know.

"My favorite flavor is orange," she said.

There's a good example. I gave her another grunt, but she continued anyway.

"But it makes my lips look funny after I eat it. Do you have a favorite flavor?"

"Um…" I pretended to give her question serious thought as I turned my head toward the entrance. Still no Heather.

"Hey," she said, trying again to capture my attention, "have you ever watched the sun come up over the ocean?"

I turned toward her on my stool as my brain disengaged from Heather-recognizance. Then it all clicked. "You're Joni!" I said, sounding like a contestant on *The $10,000 Pyramid*.

"Yeah?" she said, looking a bit confused.

I tried to walk back my sudden enthusiasm and explain. "My friend told me, um… no, you see, I saw a girl walking, um, down the street…early in the morning. Sunday."

"You did?"

"And he told me that was probably you."

"You asked about me?" she asked, sounding pleased.

"Well, sort of, yeah. I was just surprised to see somebody my age out that early in the morning."

"You think it's weird, don't you?" she asked, sheepishly.

"Oh, no. Not at all."

"Because, you know, to see me out there, you must have been up early too."

"I was. I saw you out my bedroom window." I immediately didn't like the way that sounded.

"Well, next time you get up that early, you should come out on the beach. I'll probably be out there. The sunrise is my favorite. And it's the best time to find sharks' teeth."

"Sharks?" I asked, a little surprised.

"Yeah, you know, those big fish," she said, putting her hand on her head like it was a shark fin, "with the big teeth?"

"I know what sharks are. Why are their teeth on the beach?"

"My grandpa says when they bite into little kids, they lose their teeth, and they wash up on shore. The teeth do, not the little kids. They eat those."

It sounded like her grandpa and my mom had read the same book on how to scare kids away from swimming at the beach. "They eat little kids?" I asked, playing along.

"Well, sure. That and other things. My grandpa says—"

"Hey, man!" said Joey, interrupting my marine science lesson. "Sorry I took so long."

"Hey, Joey," I said standing up from the stool.

"Is Heather here, yet?" he asked, looking around.

I gave the arcade another quick once over. "I haven't seen her. Maybe she's not coming. Or maybe she's already been here."

"Oh, well," he said with a dismissive shrug. "You wanna play some air hockey?"

"Sure," I said, as we started toward the large game table in the middle of the arcade floor.

"Dude," Joey said, "that girl you just were talking to is the sunrise girl you asked about. Joni."

"Yeah, I just figured that out," I said, glancing back at the counter. She had disappeared from the order window.

"Her family owns this place."

"Oh, well that makes sense," I said. "I was wondering why she worked here."

"And?" Joey asked as we stopped at the air hockey table.

"And, what?"

"What did you think of her?"

"Oh. She's nice, I guess," I said. "I wasn't really listening to a lot of what she was saying."

Speaking of not listening, Joey had turned his full attention to the air hockey table. "Are you any good?" he asked.

"I don't know," I said, honestly. "I've never played."

A smile grew on Joey's face. "Tell you what," he said. "I'll pay for the first game. Loser pays for the next one. Deal?"

Knowing Joey for all of five days, I was fairly confident he was setting me up to pay for all our air hockey games going forward. But not wanting to sound unconfident, I agreed. He leaned down and fed fifty cents into the slot, bringing the whole table to aerated life. He then grabbed one of the red plastic pushers floating aimlessly around the playing surface and shoved the other one to me. We took our places at each end of the table.

"Ready?" Joey asked like he was warning me of something.

"Ready," I said.

Now, I have to say here that there are times when some people are just good at things without trying. I bet when Johnny Bench was a little kid and swung at his first baseball, he probably nailed it. Unless the little kid throwing it was Vida Blue. I'm just saying some things come naturally to some people for no explainable reason. With that being said, I didn't pay for an air hockey game with Joey that whole summer.

"Wanna play again?" I asked after winning the first three games.

"Um, no," he said. "Let's try something else." He looked around before deciding on foosball.

Like air hockey, I had never played foosball before, but it didn't look hard to play. I assumed you just spin your player rods really fast until one of the men kicks the ball into the goal. Since Joey was almost out of money, I paid for our first game. As soon as I dropped the ball onto the playing surface, I started spinning all my rods like a maniac.

Joey called timeout after two seconds. "OK, that's not how you play," he said, leaning on his rod handles.

"What's wrong?" I asked, my men slowly spinning to a stop.

"You don't just stand there and spin your players," he said. "Anybody can do that. This is a skill game. My dad and I play all the time. Let me show you."

Joey proceeded to give me a lesson on ball control, passing, and shooting. He also gave me tips on playing defense. While it was helpful, what I really wanted his advice on was Heather. As we started playing again Joey's way, I asked, "So, what do I do if she comes in?"

"Who? Heather?" he asked, his eyes following the ball as it ricocheted around the table.

"Yeah."

"I don't know, why don't you buy her a snow cone or popcorn or something."

That sounded like a good plan. "Then what?" I asked.

Joey laughed and shook his head as he controlled the ball with his midfielders. "Sorry, dude, I can't help you with that."

"Why?" I asked, spinning my midfield rod.

"No spinning," said Joey, stopping the ball with one of his men.

"Sorry," I said. "You've never had a girlfriend before?"

"I'm twelve," he said, resuming play. "What do I need a girlfriend for?"

Joey seemed to have a habit of asking questions for which I had no answers. I shrugged instead.

"Look," he continued, "just don't get your hopes up, OK? Heather's…"

Instead of finishing his sentence, Joey lost himself in the flow of the game. Moving the white ball around the table with precision, he passed it to one of his three yellow men facing my defenders. With a quick slide and a flick of his wrist, he slapped the ball past my goalie so hard I blinked and missed it.

"Hah!" he said, pointing his finger at me. "One, zip!"

I retrieved another ball from underneath my goal and asked, "Heather's what?"

"Huh?" asked Joey, still enjoying his goal.

"You were about to say something about Heather."

"Oh, yeah. Look, man, she's just a girl. Don't get all bugged out about her."

"Don't you like her?"

"Ran, if you lived here, you'd know every boy likes Heather," he said, waving his hand to hurry me up. "Put the ball in play for us."

I slid the ball through the hole in the side of the table, and we started playing again. While my hands focused on stopping Joey's constant offensive attack, my mind wondered if I was in over my head with Heather.

"Just be cool, OK?" said Joey, bouncing the ball back and forth between two of his three attack men. "Remember, she's thirteen, so she's older than you. Besides, she probably won't even show."

As Joey prepared to school me again, my eyes were pulled away from the game toward the arcade entrance. He slammed the ball past my distracted goalie and shouted, "Hah! Two, zip!"

"Dude, there she is," I said.

ELEVEN

Dancing in the Moonlight

When I was in my fourth-grade math class, I sat next to a kid named Tony Sanders. Tony was always a fun kid to be around, but that was the problem. He never turned it off, even in class. His primary objective every day was to make me laugh out loud when I wasn't supposed to. Little things like looking at me with pencils hanging out of each nostril when the teacher was writing on the chalkboard. Or smiling at me with the fake zombie teeth he'd saved from Halloween while we were taking a quiz. On that occasion, my teacher sent me – not him – out into the hallway to finish my quiz. She made me pull my desk and chair outside the classroom and close the door. It was embarrassing, but once I was out there I kind of liked the privacy and lack of distractions. That is, until a class of second graders came walking down the hallway, single file, led by my mother. She was working that day as a substitute teacher. I had never been so nervous to see someone walking toward me. Until Heather Altman entered the arcade.

I saw Heather and her friend before she saw us at the foosball table. She was wearing a yellow, flowery, puffy-shoulder shirt that only covered where her white bikini top had been earlier in the day and white shorts with bare feet. Some things you just don't forget. She saw us, waved, and began heading our way leaving her friend at the snack counter. My heart began to pound in my chest. *Don't forget to breathe*, I reminded myself.

"Hey, Joey," said Heather, smiling as she saddled up to the foosball table. "Hey, Ringo."

"Hey, Heather," I said, calmly. There, I did it. I was quite proud of myself.

"It's Ran," Joey said to Heather.

"Oh, my bad," said Heather, laughing at herself. "I'm sorry, Ran!"

It took me until then to realize she had called me Ringo. At least the beagle had a cool name. So, I put on a smile and said, "It's OK."

"What are you guys up to?" she asked.

"We're playing foosball," Joey said, stating the obvious.

"But we're done, now," I added, turning away from the table to face Heather.

"No, we're not," said Joey. "We just started."

"Y'all can keep playing," she said. "We just got here."

"No, that's OK," I said. "We were just about to play air hockey, weren't we Joey?"

"No, we weren't. I want to finish our foosball game."

"I can watch," said Heather. "Go ahead and finish."

"How about I buy you a snow cone or popcorn, instead?" I offered.

Joey jumped in before Heather could answer. "He just doesn't want to keep playing because I'm beating him."

"I was letting him win," I countered, "because he couldn't beat me at air hockey."

"You weren't letting me win!" shouted Joey.

"I was too!" I shouted.

"You were not!"

"I was too!"

"Um, I'll just leave you guys alone to work things out," said Heather, backing away slowly.

We both watched her walk back to her friend at the snack counter without comment.

I turned to face Joey. "Now, see what you did?"

"What I did!?" he said. "You just wanted to show off in front of Heather!"

"Well, so did you!"

We stood glaring at each other from across the table. I looked over at Heather, who was laughing and talking with her friend. I then looked back at Joey. He was sore, I could tell. So was I. But when you're stranded on an island, you can't be too

84

picky about your friends. And I couldn't afford to lose the only one I had. I reached down and grabbed a ball from the table.

"I think you just scored," I said, calmly. "It's two, zip." I put the ball in play.

Joey let it roll past his men without moving them. I tapped the ball with one of my men and watched it roll slowly, unobstructed toward his goalie. Just before making contact, he slid his goalie out of the way and let the ball drop in for a score.

"Two, one," he said.

"Thanks," I said.

"I let you have that one," he said.

"I know, I saw that. Thank you."

"Can we play, now?" he asked.

"Sure."

We started playing again, with me actively trying to give Joey a good, competitive game. And after applying some of what he taught me, I scored my first real goal.

"Nice shot," Joey said.

"Thanks. And sorry about all that with Heather."

"Yeah. Me too."

"Friends?" I asked, stretching my hand across the table.

"Yeah, friends," he said, shaking on it.

He went on to beat me 5-2. But I only lost a game of foosball, not a friend, so I counted it as a win.

"Tell you what," Joey said after he scored the last goal, "I'm gonna make up an excuse about having to go home. You stay and hang out with Heather."

"You don't have to do that," I said.

"It's cool. I'll swing by tomorrow, and you can give me the lowdown."

We walked over to Heather who was standing next to the order window. Joni was waiting to help her.

"Who won?" Heather asked us.

"He did," we both said at the same time, pointing to each other.

She laughed. "Well, at least you guys can agree on something."

"Can I buy you a snow cone?" I asked. "I heard the orange ones are really good." I couldn't help glancing at Joni, who smiled at my recommendation.

"Yeah, I'd like that," said Heather.

I handed Joni a dollar and a minute later she had our snow cones and my change. I expected to hear more about sunrises and sharks, but this time she said nothing.

"Well, I gotta skitty," said Joey. "I've got that thing to do for my dad, for that…thing of his."

"Oh, that's right, the thing," I said, trying to support his alibi. "See you tomorrow, Joey."

As my eyes followed Joey out of the arcade, I noticed the sunlight beginning to fade. I realized I didn't tell Aunt Sarah how long I'd be gone, but I assumed it was OK to keep hanging out. It's not like I could go anywhere.

"Ran, this is my friend, Lisa," said Heather, motioning to her cute-but-less-than-Heather sidekick. "She was just leaving."

"Oh, nice to meet you, Lisa," I said with an awkward wave.

"Nice to meet you, Ran," said Lisa politely as she turned to leave. "See you back at the house, Heather."

Suddenly, we were alone. Just Heather and me and our snow cones. I was finally on a date with the same girl I'd been pining over for the last eight hours. But now what? Joey said to just be cool. *Be cool,* I told myself.

I watched Heather nibble a bit of her snow cone. She ate it from the side, just above the paper cone, which scored major points with me. Any experienced snow cone eater knows that if you eat it from the side, you get more flavor than eating off the top. I was impressed.

"Want to eat these on the beach?" she asked.

"That sounds radical," I said, cringing the moment I heard it come out of my mouth. I knew *radical* was a cool word, but I was eating a snow cone, not protesting the war. She didn't laugh or roll her eyes or anything, so I apparently got away with that one. I decided to just calm down and be a little less cool.

We walked down the steps onto the soft white sand and crossed over the tall dunes to the beach. I was just following her lead, but it seemed like she wanted to go for a walk. We hadn't said anything since we started eating our snow cones, and I felt like she was waiting for me to say something. But she beat me to it.

"Joey said you're from Columbia," she said.

"Yeah. And you're from down here."

"Yeah."

"Do you live at the beach?" I asked, hoping for a yes.

"No, I'm just staying with Lisa's family through the weekend. They have a house down the street. But I'm here all the time. All the local kids hang out here."

"Have you ever looked for sharks' teeth out here?"

She laughed. "No. Why would I do that?"

"I don't know," I said. The idea seemed cool when Joni said it. But maybe not.

She pointed up to the dunes to our left and said, "Let's sit down and eat these before they melt."

We sat down on the sloping sand and watched the waves as we quietly ate our snow cones. She sat a lot closer to me than I had expected. Not that I minded. I could feel her hip against mine as we crunched the orange ice from our cones.

"You know these orange snow cones will make our lips look funny," I said, breaking the silence.

"I think I know how to fix that," she said, turning her head to me.

I looked into her eyes as she slowly leaned over, moving her face inches from mine. She closed her eyes and tilted her head slightly. I got the distinct impression she was expecting me to do something. (This seems like an appropriate time to mention that I'd never kissed a girl before. And I wasn't exactly sure what I was supposed to do.)

Without opening her eyes, she whispered, "Aren't you going to kiss me?"

Now that she'd made the situation obvious, I puckered my lips and leaned my face into hers. She recoiled slightly and said softly, "Relax."

I loosened my lips and tried placing them gently on hers. This time, I felt her press against me. I could taste the orange snow cone on her soft, cold, wet lips. And then she changed the rules. She opened her mouth creating a hole where my lips were. I backed away, unsure of what was happening.

"Is this the first time you've kissed a girl?" she asked, still inches from my face.

"Oh, no. I've kissed...hundreds of girls," I said, hoping my answer was in the range of normal.

"Hundreds, really?" she asked, smiling.

"No," I admitted. "You're the first."

"It's OK," she said, with a comforting look in her eyes. "Let's try again. But when I open my mouth, you stick your tongue out."

I heard her, but I must have looked lost.

"Here, I'll show you," she said. "When we kiss, open your mouth like I did. Ready?"

I nodded. She pressed her lips against mine, and I opened my mouth. Her tongue moved around mine like we were shaking hands without thumbs, and then she pulled back.

"That's called French kissing," she said. "Now you try."

Without boring you with the details, let's just say Heather let me practice my new skill for quite a while there on the dunes. I'd hear other people talking as they walked by, but neither of us acknowledged their presence. I don't know how long my eyes were closed, but when she finally pulled her face away, the beach was almost dark.

I looked at the beautiful lips I'd been kissing and chuckled at what I saw. The orange dye from the snow cone had smeared all around her mouth.

"What's so funny?" she asked, smiling.

"You've got orange all around your mouth."

"Oh, my god," she said looking at my face. "So do you! I look like that?"

"I guess so," I said, sensing a bit of panic on her part.

"I've got to go," she said, rising to her feet.

"You want to go back inside King's?" I asked, getting up from the sand.

"Are you kidding?" she asked, brushing off her shorts. "I can't go anywhere like this. Somebody might see me."

"I can walk you back to your house," I said, trying to be a gentleman.

"God, no. We can't be seen together like this. People will know what we've been doing."

"I'm OK with that," I said with a smile.

She huffed. "Just give me a head start. You stay here for a minute. And please stay out of King's with that orange on your face."

I watched her hurry away down the beach and up through the dunes.

"Bye," I shouted after her. "See you tomorrow!"

I sat back down on the base of the sand dune. Waves rolled in before me, their white foam glowing in the moonlight. *Heather kissed me.* The thought floated around and around inside my otherwise empty mind. I laid back on the sand, folded my hands together on my chest, and smiled at the stars in the darkening sky. *Heather kissed me.*

TWELVE

The Morning After

A firm knock on my bedroom door jolted me out of a dead sleep. I had been dreaming that I was at King's. Heather was feeding Ringo an orange snow cone while they both watched Joni beat Joey in air hockey. I opened my eyes to see Uncle Breland, harbinger of reality, standing in my open doorway. A feeling of panic filled my body as I feared that my date with Heather had simply been a dream. I ignored my uncle's presence and scrambled to the bathroom to look in the mirror. There it was. The beautiful orange snow cone stain all around the smile on my face. It really happened. A wonderful feeling of relief sent me staggering back into my room to fall limply onto my bed.

"When you finish whatever it is you're doing," said Uncle Breland, "put on some clothes and come downstairs."

"Can I eat, first?" I asked.

"I wouldn't, but that's just me," he said leaving the doorway.

Aunt Sarah appeared after Uncle Breland left. "I have a surprise for you in the kitchen, Ran," she said. "Whenever you're ready."

I was always ready for a surprise, especially when it came to my aunt Sarah's cooking. What amazing creation was waiting for me to devour? Blueberry pancakes? Cinnamon French toast? Waffles? Biscuits and gravy? I hopped off the bed and back into the bathroom to wash the orange off my face before stepping into the kitchen. But I didn't smell anything cooking or frying.

Aunt Sarah reached into the cabinet next to the refrigerator and retrieved something which she then hid behind her back. "I found this at the IGA Foodliner in Litchfield yesterday," she said. She smiled as she revealed a box of Captain Crunch with Crunch Berries.

"Oh, wow!" I said, taking the box into my hands. "Thank you, Aunt Sarah!" While I was happy to be holding my favorite cereal, a tinge of disappointment forced me to fake some of my enthusiasm. Aunt Sarah had officially raised the bar for breakfast. Nevertheless, I filled a big bowl with milk and cereal and reverted to my old Captain Crunch self.

"What's downstairs?" I asked her.

"Your uncle caught some fish yesterday," she explained as she poured herself a cup of coffee, "and I'm going to cook them for our supper. He just needs your help, I think."

"Oh, OK," I said, slurping the cereal off my spoon. At least it wasn't yardwork again.

The treasure hunt was gone from the back of the cereal box, so I had nothing else to do but eat. I finished a lot faster than usual and, with a quick change into shorts and a t-shirt, I was ready to head down the front steps.

"Don't forget to brush your teeth," my aunt called out behind me.

"I won't," I shouted back to her. Although, technically, I could remember to do it the next day or the next week and still be good on my promise. Adults should be more specific with things like that.

I hadn't been inside the downstairs part of the house, so I was a little cautious as I opened the screen door and called for Uncle Breland.

"Back here," he said, leaving me to figure out the rest.

The rooms were arranged differently than those upstairs. There was no den, just three bedrooms, one filled with boxes, on either side of a narrow hallway. I followed the nauseating smell of dead fish to the kitchen in the back. Uncle Breland was standing at a wooden table, holding a large knife in his hand. It wasn't the most comforting image, so I eased slowly into the room.

"Hey, Uncle Breland," I said.

"You ever clean a fish before?" he asked, placing the knife on the table next to a large cooler.

"No, sir," I answered. I hoped that would exempt me from whatever he had in mind.

"Come over here. See those fish in that cooler?"

"Yes, sir."

"You're going to clean those so your aunt can cook them for our supper tonight."

I wasn't really sure what he meant by "clean" or what the knife had to do with it, but I agreed anyway. "OK. How do I do that?"

"That's what I'm going to show you. Now pay attention." He took a dead fish from the cooler and plopped it on the table in front of me. "This is a speckled trout," he said, picking up the knife. "You've also got a few redfish in there. But here's how you clean a trout."

He pointed the knife to what he called the anal fin on the fish's belly. When I giggled, he said, "Fish poop too, you know." He then stabbed the knife into the fish, giving me play-by-play as he went.

"You take the knife and cut right down to the anal fin until you hit the backbone. Then turn the knife and cut along the backbone until you hit the gills."

As I watched him butcher the fish, I started to feel something happening in my stomach. Something not good.

"Once you hit the gills, flip it sideways. Got that?" he asked.

I nodded yes and tried not to breathe the aroma of dead fish and stale cigarette smoke that filled the small kitchen. The feeling in my stomach had turned into a rumbling and was beginning to move north.

"Then slide the knife down and hit the backbone again." He paused and looked at me. "You OK, Turtle?"

Before I could get any words out, my breakfast beat me to it, fire-hosing from my mouth into the cooler full of fish. When the violence was over, I held onto the table for a moment to support my wobbly legs while I tried to recompose myself. I was afraid to turn my head and look up at Uncle Breland. But out of the corner of my eye, I saw the knife drop onto the table. The sound of his feet heading down the hallway and the slam of the screen door told me I was alone.

I waited there in the kitchen, trying to decide what to do. Maybe I should clean up after myself, I thought. I peered into the cooler at the fish swimming in a sea of Captain Crunch and milk and almost threw up again. I backed away from the table and staggered toward the front of the house. Before I made it to the porch, I heard someone coming down the stairs outside. It was Uncle Breland. He stomped over to his pickup truck, got in, and drove away. I figured it was safe to go upstairs.

"Ran?" I heard Aunt Sarah say from the kitchen as I let the screened porch door close behind me. "Are you OK, honey?"

I met her in the den. "Yes, ma'am," I said. "I just got sick."

"I heard," she said, with a consoling smile.

"Where's Uncle Breland?"

"He went to catch us some more fish for dinner."

"Oh, I guess that's my fault," I said.

She put her hand on my forehead and told me not to worry about the fish. After pouring me a glass of iced tea, she told me just to sit on the porch for a while and let my stomach settle. I did as I was told while she went downstairs to clean up my mess. I felt bad, not so much physically, but more in a guilty way. I had been trying to stay below my uncle's radar and not create any problems or burdens for my aunt. But now, because of me, they were both doing things they didn't want to do, while I sat alone on their porch.

After a little while, Aunt Sarah made her way back upstairs and joined me. I apologized for the mess and asked if there was anything I could do, but she told me just to relax. We rocked together quietly for a little while before she asked me about my night at King's.

"Oh, it was good," I said, trying not to sound too enthusiastic. "Fun, I mean."

"What did you do down there?"

I told her how good I was at air hockey and how good Joey was at foosball. And how good the orange snow cones were.

"I saw two pretty girls about your age walking down the street toward King's last night after you left," she said.

"You did?" I asked, wondering where she was going with that.

"Mm-mm. And then I saw your friend Joey walking home, but you weren't with him."

"Oh, he had a thing to go do. That's why he left."

"I see. So, did you make any new friends last night?"

Wow. When it came to deductive reasoning, Fred and Velma had nothing on Aunt Sarah. "New friends?" I replied, innocently, hoping to throw her off the trail.

"Mm-mm," she said, knowingly.

Just like a villain in *Scooby-Doo*, I confessed rather easily. "Well, there is this one girl," I said. Before I could go any further, Joey appeared on the street below walking toward our house. Relieved and thankful for the distraction, I called out his name. He looked up at us and waved.

"Hey man," he said. "I'm going out on the beach, wanna come?"

"Is that OK, Aunt Sarah?" I asked.

I could tell she was disappointed with the interruption. But she nodded and said, "As long as you feel up to it."

"I'm fine," I said, getting up from my chair.

"Did you ever brush your teeth?" she asked.

Shoot. I hadn't, but maybe it was a good idea, considering. "I'll be down in just a minute, Joey," I shouted.

After brushing my teeth, putting on a bathing suit, and grabbing the last of my Nekots, I made it down to the street to meet Joey.

"And stay out of the water," my aunt added from the porch.

"Yes, ma'am!" I shouted, before asking Joey, "What's up?"

"Not much," he said, turning to walk up the street.

The cloudless morning was hotter than I expected, and the pavement was already warm on my bare feet. I moved over into the sand and took my chances with sandspurs.

"Wanna go to the south end?" asked Joey.

"Sure, I guess," I said. I didn't know why one end of the island would be better or different than the other, but I assumed Joey had his reasons. "What's down there?"

"You'll see," he said. "So, how'd it go with Heather last night?"

"Good," I said, repeating the answer I gave Aunt Sarah. I could tell from Joey's face that he was expecting something more. "What?" I asked.

"That's it? It was good? Nothing else?"

I was new to the whole girlfriend thing and wasn't sure how much I was supposed to tell people, so I thought it best to keep it simple. "No, that's it," I said. "So, what's at the south end?"

"It's a surprise," he said frowning at me.

After the fish-cleaning incident, I wasn't up for any more surprises that morning, so I offered Joey an incentive. "Will you tell me now if I give you a cookie?"

"Nekots!" he said taking one.

"So, what's down there?"

He put a whole cookie in his mouth and, as far as I could tell, he said, "We're going to the other side."

"Other side of what?" I asked.

"The creek. I heard there's a big saltwater pond on the DeBordieu side behind the dunes that you can swim in."

That sounded cool, but we were walking north toward King's and away from the beach access path. "Isn't the south end that way?" I asked pointing behind us.

"That's part of the surprise. I thought we'd walk by Lisa's house and see if she and Heather want to go with us."

"Oh," I said, a little off guard. I hadn't mentally prepared myself to spend the morning with Heather. I'd been too busy basking in the glow of our snow-cone-beach-kiss to think of what I would say the next time I saw her.

"That's OK, isn't it?" he asked.

"Sure," I said, cautiously.

"What's wrong? She's not mad at you or anything is she?"

"Why would she be mad at me?"

"I don't know. I thought maybe you destroyed her in air hockey or something."

"No, we didn't play air hockey," I said, smiling on the inside.

"What did y'all do?" he asked, leading us across the street.

I followed Joey to the same beach path that led past Mr. Wilson's house. "I don't think we should go this way," I said.

"Why not?"

"The man who lives in that house yelled at me for getting on his dunes."

"Oh, that's just Old Man Wilson. He yells at everybody."

"My aunt told me to stay away from him," I said.

"Probably because he murdered his wife."

"He what?!"

"That's what I heard," said Joey. "And he's hiding her dead body in his house somewhere."

"Are you serious?"

"Sure. No one's seen her in years. Ask anybody. And the old fart got away with it."

I shook my head. "Why are all the old men on this island so cranky?"

"I don't know. I guess that's what living at the beach does to you," he said, pointing ahead of us. "Heather's staying in that house right there."

We stopped beside a house on the row behind Mr. Wilson's. We could see Lisa sitting in a rocking chair on the front porch. Joey waved to get her attention.

"You guys wanna walk to the south end?" he called out.

Lisa looked to her right for a moment, then back at us. "We can't. My mom's taking us to the Hammock Shop in a little while."

"Ten-four!" said Joey. "Tell Heather we stopped by."

"I'll tell her," said Lisa with a wave.

Joey gave me a pat on the shoulder. "Sorry, dude. I tried."

I wasn't too disappointed. I was sure I would see her later.

As we turned toward the dunes, we could see Mr. Wilson standing on his deck, his arms folded as he looked out over the beach. He turned and watched us climb to the top of the dunes like he was memorizing our faces for a police sketch artist. Joey waved to him as we ran down the other side. Mr. Wilson unfolded his arms and placed his hands on his hips as he watched us laugh our way onto the beach. He wasn't happy. We jogged down to the water line and turned toward the pier.

"That guy's scary!" I said, slowing to a walk.

"So, you're really not going to tell me what you and Heather did last night?" Joey asked.

"I don't think I'm supposed to talk about that stuff. She's my girlfriend, now," I said, trying out the g-word for the first time.

"Whoa!" Joey said, with a laugh, grabbing my arm. "Does Heather know about this?"

"What does that mean?" I asked, pulling my arm free.

"Why do you think Heather's your girlfriend?"

I quickly decided the need to mount a solid defense outweighed the need for privacy. "Because," I said, "we kissed on the beach last night."

Joey laughed. "Is that it?"

"Yeah," I said, still sure of myself. "But it was for a long time."

"You kissed for a long time," he summarized for me. "Anything else?"

"No," I said, resting my case.

"Did she say anything?"

I thought for a second, quickly playing back our time together. "No, not really," I said, "We didn't talk much."

Joey shook his head. "You don't have a girlfriend," he said, definitively.

"Yes, I do."

"No, you don't"

"Yes, I do."

"No, you don't."

How could he know that? I was the one who kissed her, not him. I kept my eyes on the sand beneath my feet and shook my head.

"Look," he said as we walked beneath the pier, "it's just Heather being Heather. I told you she wasn't like other girls."

Since I didn't know what other girls were like, necessarily, that wasn't helpful. "But why would she kiss me if she doesn't like me?" I asked.

Joey laughed as if he'd thought of a joke. "Maybe she was just practicing," he said.

"Practicing for what?" I asked, totally serious.

Joey turned his head and gave me a look. "Geez, Ran. Didn't your dad ever sit you down and talk to you about s-e-x?"

My eyebrows pushed downward as I considered the question for a moment. "No," I admitted. "Did yours?"

"Sure," he said. "All dads do. It's like part of their job or something."

I'm not saying it was intentional, but everything Joey talked about seemed to have a dad reference. My dad *this* or my dad *that*. Like I needed a reminder that I rarely had a reason to say my dad *anything*.

"Stupid coffee," I muttered under my breath.

"What?" asked Joey.

"Nothing," I said.

I tried to offer a quick cover story for my dad. "My dad's just real busy. I'm sure he'll get around to it. He owns a coffee shop, you know."

"Anyway," said Joey, moving on, "just don't get too hung up on Heather. Or look, if you really want a girlfriend, what about Joni? She digs you, man. I can tell."

"The girl at King's? You said she was weird!"

"No, I didn't."

"Yes, you did."

After a moment of reflection, Joey admitted, "OK, maybe I did say that. But it was just about the sunrise thing. She's a nice girl."

Granted, Joni did seem nice. But we were comparing apples and oranges. "Joni's like a little girl compared to Heather," I said, confidently.

Joey laughed and shook his head. "I hate to break this to you man, but you're twelve!"

I tried to think of a decent comeback to that, but I had nothing. It wasn't the first time Joey left me with nothing to say. I knew he was wrong about Heather, but he seemed to know more than me about girls, diving off piers, foosball, crabbing, s-e-x, and pretty much everything else. So, rather than pursue a debate I might lose, I turned my attention to the beach.

"So, how far is it to the south end?" I asked.

"I don't know," said Joey. He lifted his arm and pointed. "It's just down there. A couple miles I guess."

"We're walking a couple of miles?" I asked.

"What else do you have to do?"

He'd done it again.

THIRTEEN

Drift Away

As far as walking along the shore goes, Pawleys Island felt like two different beaches. North of the pier, where my aunt and uncle's house sat, the beach was wide, flat, and open. You could run all around, throw a ball as far as you could, ride a bike on the sand to the north inlet, and do pretty much anything you wanted. It was like a big oceanfront park, especially at low tide. But once Joey and I crossed under the pier heading south, the beach became divided into sections by what he called groins. Starting just below the dunes, the groins were long, thick, wooden fences that rose from the sand and stretched out into the ocean. And there were about twenty of them between us and the south end. The result was what seemed like a series of fenced-off mini-beaches. Several groins had giant boulders on either side, supporting the wooden planks, some of which looked rotten or were altogether missing in some sections.

Joey and I couldn't resist climbing onto the groins' wooden spines and walking their length tightrope-style. Immune from the ocean current and thrashing of the waves, it felt like we were walking on the water. And once we reached the quiet isolation waiting at the end, we could look back toward shore, the length of the island visible to us from north to south. But after conquering the first few groins, Joey suggested we skip the rest and head on to the creek.

Since talking about girls had proven fruitless, our conversation naturally turned to music as we passed the blaring radios of people lounging on the beach. Joey liked rock bands like The Rolling Stones, The Steve Miller Band, Steely Dan, and Lynyrd Skynyrd. But he was particularly obsessed with a new song called *Rock On* by some guy named David Essex. It was one of the weirdest, most pointless songs I'd ever heard on the radio. When I expressed my opinion about that, Joey stopped on the sand, whipped out his invisible guitar, and shouted (with eyes closed tightly, of course), "Jimmy Dean! Jimmy Dean! Rock On! Rock On!" While I enjoyed laughing at how ridiculous Joey looked, I still didn't get the song at all.

As for me, I tended to focus more on songs that I liked rather than the artists who sang them. I did have a few exceptions to that rule of course. Olivia (obviously), The Monkees, The Jackson Five, and the late Jim Croce, whose mention led us into a loud, spontaneous rendition of the chorus from his song *You Don't Mess Around With Jim*. Ignoring the stares and smiles from people passing by, we laughed together at our performance. Although, we did get into a brief debate on whether you should say Jim or Slim at the end. I said Jim since that was the name of the song. Joey insisted we should say Slim since Slim beat up Jim. We agreed to disagree.

I'm not sure how long it took us, but we finally arrived at the south end. The beach had become narrow as we made our way past the last set of groins. A single row of houses to our right sat squished between the ocean and the creek behind them. Once past the houses, the south end of Pawleys was nothing but a round sandy beach, capping the island like an eraser on the end of a pencil. The creek flowed slowly toward the ocean while a few people wandered around aimlessly looking for things on the sand.

As we got closer to the creek, Joey picked up the pace a bit. And of course, that's the exact moment my mom's shark-alligator-stingray-jellyfish-oyster-shell creek warning invaded my conscience. "Hey," I said, trying to slow our pace, "I forgot, I'm not supposed to get in the water."

Joey didn't slow down. He just turned around to face me while jogging backward. "That didn't seem to stop you on the pier, did it?" he asked, with a shrug.

He had a point, but the pier was different. There was a girl involved.

"Come on, let's go!" he said. With that, Joey turned and broke into a full sprint. He leapt from the sandy bank, splashing headfirst into the creek's smooth green water. At least he actually dove in this time, I thought.

I offered a quick verbal apology to my mother, picked up some speed, and followed Joey's example. For some reason, I enjoyed the short running dive into the creek more than my death-defying leap off the pier. When my face surfaced in the cool water, I felt a burst of new energy. I even let out a loud, touristy, "Woo!" Sometimes it's good to be where no one knows you.

We swam across the creek, floating along with the tide's current until it was shallow enough to stand. I waded out to the other side as Joey waited for me to catch up.

"I think the pond's just on the other side of those big dunes over there," he said, pointing upward.

The dunes were much taller than those on Pawleys. There were no houses behind them either. The whole beach seemed like undiscovered territory. We climbed our way to the top of the dunes and looked down the other side. About twenty feet below was a dark green, egg-shaped pond about half the size of a regular swimming pool.

"I told ya!" said Joey.

"How long has this been here?" I asked, wondering how it got there in the first place.

"I don't know. Who cares? We have our own swimming pool!"

I could tell Joey was just a little excited.

"Do you think there's anything in it?" I asked. "Like alligators or...alligators?" I couldn't think of any other man-eating animals likely to be swimming around down there.

"Only one way to find out," Joey said, his eyebrows raised waiting for my reply.

Despite my reservations, I'd walked two miles and swam across a possibly shark-infested creek against my mother's wishes for this. So, I gave a nodding smile and raced him down the hill. We hit the water at the same time, with Joey diving and me running in, splashing until I fell. Then it was a race to see how fast we could get back out. The water was boiling hot. Well, not literally. But way too hot to swim in.

With both of us back on dry sand a few seconds later, I shouted the obvious, "That was hot!"

"I know!" said Joey. "Now I know how our boiled crabs feel."

"It kinda smells funny too," I said, sniffing my wet arm. "Who told you about this?"

Joey stood with his hands on his hips facing the pool. "I heard some older kids talking in the store a few days ago," he said. "I thought it sounded cool. But it's definitely not."

"Nope," I agreed.

He looked away from me and spit. "I think those dudes faked me out on purpose."

"You really think so?"

"Yeah. That's OK, though. Payback will be fun." He turned and started up the dune.

"What are you going to do?" I asked climbing the sand next to him.

"I don't know, yet. But we'll think of something."

I didn't really like the "we" part of that, but I didn't push back either. When we reached the top of the dune we sat down. From our elevated perch, we could see all the way to the Pawleys pier and the creek winding its way through the marsh. On the back side of the island, around the bend from where we dove into the creek, a few men sat on the sand holding fishing poles over the water. As I tried to see if one of them might be Uncle Breland, Joey asked me a question.

"So, why'd you want to spend your summer down here instead of at home?"

"I didn't," I said. "At first, I mean. Now I'm not minding it so much."

"So, your folks made you come down here?"

"Yeah. My dad, mostly."

"What's he like?"

"My dad? He's, um…" I thought for a moment, unsure how to answer. "You know, he's just a regular dad, I guess."

"Why'd he want you to come down here?"

"He's always busy working. So, they sent me down here. Just to get me out of the way, I think."

"That stinks," said Joey.

"Yeah."

"What about your mom?" he asked.

I shrugged my shoulders. "She just went along with it. My uncle said she dumped me on the beach like a sea turtle. I don't really know what that means, but that's what he calls me now. Turtle."

"Momma sea turtles lay their eggs on the beach and then swim away," Joey explained. "That's why he calls you that."

"Oh. Does she come back?"

"Nope."

"What happens to the baby turtles when they hatch from their eggs?"

"They just fend for themselves," said Joey. "Some of 'em get eaten by birds before they can make it to the water."

"That's all starting to make sense now."

"So, watch out for those seagulls, man," Joey said, grinning.

"Very funny."

We sat quietly for a minute or two, just taking in everything around us. The saltwater pool was a bust, but having our own hilltop to sit on, away from everyone else was pretty cool.

"I like it up here," Joey said. "Kinda helps you forget about things for a minute."

"What kind of things?" I asked, unsure what he meant.

"We should head back," he said, ignoring my question. "I've got to work later this afternoon."

"OK," I said, as we rose to our feet.

We slid our way down the front side of the dune and turned toward the creek. Walking along the beach, I happened to see what looked like a shiny black vampire tooth. "Hey, look at this," I said, picking it up.

"That's a shark's tooth," said Joey. "This is a good place to find them. There's never anybody over here."

"Want to look for more of these?" I asked, hoping for some experienced help.

"Nah, I'd better go."

I examined the tooth resting in the palm of my hand, fascinated with the idea that it came out of a shark's mouth. "This is far out," I said. "I think I'm gonna stay and look for more."

"All right. I'll check you later," said Joey, beginning to leave. "But don't wait too long. Tide's going out."

"OK," I said, with a wave. I didn't really know at the time why he told me about the tide, but I would soon find out.

As I scanned the sand for more teeth, I noticed Joey walking up the creek shoreline away from the beach and wondered where he was going. It was further up the creek from where we crossed earlier. Maybe he was looking for sharks' teeth on his way back, I thought. As the creek began to curve around the back of Pawleys, Joey finally dove in and began swimming across.

I walked down near the ocean shoreline where the waves had left little puddles on the beach. All kinds of shells, most broken into little pieces, lay scattered on the sand. More sharks' teeth had to be hiding in there somewhere, I thought. I wandered around the beach moving shells with my toes and sifting through them with my fingers until I managed to find two more. One was just another long, black, curved dagger-looking thing about a half-inch long. The other was about the same size, but it was gray, not as shiny, and more like a triangle. That one was my favorite.

Three sharks' teeth seemed like a good haul for my first try, so I decided it was time to swim back over to Pawleys. As I approached the creek, I saw the King's Funland girl, Joni, on the other side wandering around looking down at the sand. I had to assume she was tooth-hunting too. The idea of comparing our sharks' teeth seemed fun, so I started on a path directly for her.

As I waded into the water, the creek seemed a lot shallower than when we swam over, which was good. I could just walk across and not feel like I'd betrayed my mom's wishes again. But the current flowing out toward the ocean was moving much faster than I remembered. With each step forward, the soft sand below me moved sideways under my feet, carrying me slowly toward the mouth of the creek. Still, I felt like I was making progress toward the other side. So, I gripped my sharks' teeth tighter, leaned into the current, and pressed on. That's when I heard Joni.

"Help! Help!" she yelled running away up the creek shoreline, her arm pointing back in my direction.

"What's she yelling about?" I wondered out loud. I was fine. Getting across was just taking a little longer than I thought it would. I didn't need rescuing. But just a few seconds later, my opinion about that began to change. The water was getting deeper. And leaning my body into the current had my chin just about even with the surface. And my feet gained no leverage against the moving sand beneath me.

I looked toward the shore and saw Uncle Breland, of all people, sprinting along the creek shore. My first thought was, "I didn't know he could move that fast." He dove into the creek and began running in the current toward me. Up until that moment, I hadn't felt afraid of what was happening. But the look of absolute horror and desperation on my uncle's face changed that. Just as my feet began to lose contact with the sandy bottom, he reached out and grabbed my arm.

"I got you, Bobby!" he said, breathlessly.

As he dug his feet into the bottom while holding my arm, my entire body floated to the surface like a kite in the wind. His tight grip on my wrist, just below my clenched fist, began to hurt as he pulled me against the current. I could've held onto his arm to make things easier, but that would have meant dropping my sharks' teeth. And I needed to show those to Joni. I admit, the priorities of a twelve-year-old can be debatable sometimes.

Slowly, with great effort, Uncle Breland pulled me out of the current. Once we reached the shallows, he let go of my arm and we walked together from the water. He plopped down on the wet sand facing the creek, breathing heavily. I sat down next to him.

"Thank you," I said, quietly. He didn't respond at all. He just sat there, staring straight ahead at the fast-moving water. So, I moved on to the next topic on my mind and asked, "Who's Bobby?"

His head spun toward me. "What?!"

I was a little startled by his reaction, so I tried to explain. "When you grabbed me in the water, you said, 'I got you, Bobby.'"

My uncle looked away from me. After a moment, I leaned forward a bit and saw tears beginning to mix with the salt water on his face.

"Is something wrong, Uncle Breland?" I asked.

He turned and looked at me, his water-filled green eyes fixed on mine. His voice quivered as he spoke. "You don't say one word about this to anyone. Is that clear?"

I felt tears welling up in my own eyes as I looked into his. I didn't understand what was happening. "Yes, sir," I said, my lip shaking.

"Not your dad, not your aunt, not your mother, no one. Understand?"

"Yes, sir," I said, with tears flowing down my face. "I'm sorry, Uncle Breland."

My uncle shifted his weight away from me and pushed himself to his feet. He said nothing else before walking away. I sat there by myself quietly crying.

As I began to gather myself, I heard footsteps behind me. I looked up to see Joni. She sat down next to me without saying anything. I did my best to hide my tears, thankful that my face was already wet. "Hi," I said, sniffing.

"Hi," she said. "Are you OK?"

I nodded. "I'm fine."

We sat there quietly, just looking at the creek, until I finally remembered what started the whole ordeal. "Here," I said, opening my hand before her. "I found these."

She looked at the sharks' teeth in my hand, moving them around with her finger. "Those are good ones," she said. "I like the gray one best."

"Me too."

"One time I found one like that this big!" she said holding her fingers an inch apart. "I'll show it to you sometime."

"That would be cool," I said.

She pointed at the gray tooth in my hand. "You should give that one to Heather," she suggested.

"Oh," I said, surprised to hear Heather's name. "I don't think she cares about sharks' teeth."

Joni shrugged and looked at me. "Her loss," she said.

"Yeah," I said, not sure whose side I was on.

She rose to her feet. "Well, I've got to go. I have to be at the arcade in a little while."

"Oh, um, OK," I said, standing up.

"Bye," she said, beginning to walk away.

I tried to think of something, anything, to say. "Can I walk with you?" I asked.

"I rode my bike," she said, continuing her path away from me.

"Thanks for calling for help!" I said, loud enough for her to hear.

"You're welcome!" she said over her shoulder.

"Can I come buy a snow cone later?" I shouted.

She stopped and turned around. "For you or for somebody else?"

I wasn't sure why, but I liked the question. "Just for me, this time," I said.

"Then, yes." She smiled and walked away.

I watched her get on her bike and ride slowly out of sight down the street. When she was gone, I stood there alone taking in my surroundings. Just like before, a scattering of people walked around the south end aimlessly looking for things on the sand, like nothing had ever happened. But something had happened. I just wasn't sure what it was.

FOURTEEN

Sunshine On My Shoulders

Being about halfway through *Where the Red Fern Grows*, I'd been struck by how often I'd read of Billy's first-time experiences. His first coon dogs. His first coon hunting adventure. The first time his dogs treed a raccoon. His first coon hat. The first time he saw a man die over a raccoon argument. While my life didn't revolve around raccoons, thankfully, my time at the beach was also full of firsts. My first time picking up a crab. My first time diving off anything higher than the side of Michael Aston's backyard pool. The first time I kissed a girl. The first and hopefully last time I almost drowned. My first time driving (I'll tell you about that later). And my first time taking a long walk alone on a beach.

I was two miles from the house. Joey had gone home. Joni had ridden away on her bike. And waiting at the south end while Uncle Breland fished all day, just so I could ride home in his dirty pick-up truck, wasn't part of my thought process. So, I turned north and began my walk home alone.

It was well after noon, and the three Nekots I ate to replace my refunded Captain Crunch were just a distant memory. I was hungry. And as I strolled past the first groin, I knew Aunt Sarah's kitchen was a full thirty minutes away. Planning my lunch while I walked seemed like a productive use of my time. I hadn't grown tired of crunchy PB&Js yet, so they were always a possibility. Or I could just eat another bowl of the Captain since my first one didn't count. Or maybe Aunt Sarah had something even better waiting for me. But as I kept walking, my thoughts drifted away from my empty stomach and wandered on to other things. With the pier in sight the whole way, here's a short list of things I pondered while I walked:

1. What if I hadn't thrown up on Uncle Breland's fish? The only reason he was even at the creek was to catch more fish to replace the ones I ralphed on. So, if I had skipped breakfast and cleaned the fish before I went with Joey, who would have saved me in the creek? Anyone?

2. Why did Uncle Breland call me Bobby? Did he just forget my name? Why did he cry when I asked him about it? And why can't I tell anyone what happened?

3. What if Joni hadn't told me about sharks' teeth? Would I have stayed behind on DeBordieu to look for more teeth? Or would I have just crossed the creek safely with Joey?

4. Why do Crunch Berries only come in one flavor? And couldn't they just fill a whole box with Crunch Berries instead of making me dig through regular Captain Crunch to get at them?

5. When will I see Heather again? And how do I act when I'm around her? I've never had a girlfriend before. What if we're in King's and she wants a snow cone? Do I buy one for her but tell Joni it's for someone else? Then what if Joni sees Heather eating it? Will I not be able to buy snow cones for the rest of the summer?

6. Who's cuter? Heather or Joni? No question.

7. Who do I like more? Heather or Joni? Joni did help rescue me, and she is easy to talk to. But Heather is…Heather.

After crossing under the pier, I felt like I was finally back on my island again. With the groins all behind me and the tide all the way out, the beach was as wide as a football field. And if I could just remember where to cross over the dunes to the street without getting yelled at, I could make my way back to the house. While searching for my beach exit, I began to have the surprising realization that I had actually enjoyed the solitary walk back. I didn't have answers to most of the questions I had batted around but having uninterrupted time to think about them felt...good. "Oh no," I thought, "I hope I'm not growing up or something."

FIFTEEN

Tell Me Something Good

As I crossed the street after coming off the beach, the three sharks' teeth in the palm of my hand held my full attention. My brain was still spinning around questions like: How big were the sharks they came from? Why was one gray and the other two black? And did the sharks really lose them while eating little kids? As I lost myself in thought, the mailman driving toward me was nice enough not to run me over. He stopped, gave me a wave, and let me pass in front of him. But his little white mail truck did pull my mind away from sharks and send it back a few years. It's funny what can jog a memory.

When I was nine, near the end of my third-grade school year, my dad closed his coffee shop for Memorial Day. He usually closed on national holidays, the obvious ones like the Fourth of July, Christmas, Easter, Thanksgiving, and…actually, I think that was it. But he usually spent those days in his café doing things he couldn't do when it was open, rather than spending time with my mom and me. But on that day in 1971, he didn't go into the café at all. He was home all day. So, what did he do that was so memorable? He spent most of the morning and afternoon, sitting at our dining room table, writing a letter to my uncle Breland. I don't know what it was about. But every time I asked if he wanted to do something, he'd say, "In a little while," and just keep writing. He did take a break to grill some burgers in our backyard for lunch, while I played on my swing set (until my mom called me inside to help her set the table). But as far as spending time with me on his one true day off, it didn't happen. And I remembered that. Thanks, Mr. Mailman.

When I arrived back at the house, my aunt greeted me just as I hoped she would.

"Are you hungry?" she asked as I jogged up the stairs to join her on the porch.

"Yes, ma'am," I said with enthusiasm.

"Well, I forgot to buy grape jam at the store," she said, as I took a seat next to her, "but I can make you a peanut butter and banana sandwich instead. How does that sound?"

"Sounds good to me," I said. Honestly, it sounded gross. But Aunt Sarah had earned my trust in the kitchen, so I took my chances.

"Oh, and this came for you in the mail," she said, handing me an envelope. It was addressed to "Master Thomas Ransom Fox, Jr." The return address was our house in Columbia.

"I think it's from your dad," said Aunt Sarah. "I recognize his handwriting."

I sat looking at the envelope in my hands without opening it.

"I'll go make your lunch," she said, heading for the kitchen.

I'd written a few letters to Santa in my day, but I'd never received one before from anyone. The thought of my dad spending hours at the dining room table writing me a letter made me a little nervous. What could it possibly say? After sitting on that question for a minute, I decided to find out. Here's what I read, alone there on the porch:

Hey Son!

How are things at the beach? I'm sure you're enjoying your aunt Sarah's cooking. Guess who stopped into the cafe Monday? Your English teacher from last year, Ms. Edwards. She just retired after 32 years of teaching and was here with her family. When she told me who she was, we figured out that I had her for English when I was in fourth grade at Schneider School! How about that? She didn't know your uncle Breland. He was before her time. But she said to tell you hello and that she hopes you're reading a lot while you're at the beach. She made a joke about predicates which I didn't get, so I won't pass that along.

I hope you're finding lots of things to do there, ~~besides~~ including reading. If you get bored, Aunt Sarah can be nice to talk to. And if you run out of things to do or read, and Aunt Sarah's not around, you can always, as an absolute last resort, talk to your uncle Breland. You know I'm just kidding. Please tell him I said hello.

Your mom has found Pepper taking naps on your bed. I think he misses you. Be a good boy.

Love,
Dad

For all the build-up in my mind before I opened it, the payoff just wasn't there. I hoped his letter to Uncle Breland was a lot longer than mine was. As I folded the paper and stuffed it back into the envelope, Aunt Sarah returned with my lunch.

"Here you go," she said, handing me my sandwich on a plate. "What did your father have to say?"

I took a bite of my sandwich like Pepper devouring a piece of crispy bacon. I'd get to Aunt Sarah's question in a minute. But first, I had to catch up with what I had just stuffed into my mouth. It was chewy, crunchy, peanut buttery, and banana-ie. I would've eaten anything at that moment, but what filled my cheeks was amazing. Peanut butter and bananas. I was sold.

Aunt Sarah waited patiently for my answer, then realized she hadn't brought me anything to drink. "Oh! I'm sorry," she said rushing off to the kitchen while I chewed. She came back with a cold bottle of Pepsi. I was all set.

After taking a swig, I wiped my mouth with the back of my hand and said, "Not much."

"Not much?" she asked.

"Not really. He just said something about my teacher from school."

"Oh," she said, thoughtfully. She rocked for a moment in her chair. "Your father writes beautiful letters. I'm surprised he didn't say more than that."

"No, that was it," I said, not knowing enough to share in her surprise.

"Your grandfather used to write letters to your uncle. He's kept them all."

"I never met my grandfather," I said.

"Well, you did, but you were just a baby. He passed away shortly after you were born. I imagine your father has kept some letters from him too. You should ask him about that."

"Didn't they have telephones back then?" I asked.

My aunt chuckled as she rocked. "Yes, we had telephones. But sometimes you just have things you need to say in writing. Words can mean so much more that way."

I opened the envelope and read the letter again as I ate my sandwich. Maybe I was missing something, but I didn't see anything meaningful, other than the fact that my dog misses me. If my dad really needed to tell me that, I guess the ten-cent stamp was cheaper than a long-distance phone call. Maybe that's what he was thinking.

"When you finish your sandwich," my aunt said, "I want you to run something over to Ms. Mary's house."

"The hair lady in the trailer?" I asked.

She smiled and nodded at my question. "Can you do that for me?"

I had planned to walk over to King's after I ate and get my snow cone from Joni, but I could do that afterward. "Yes, ma'am," I said.

When I'd finished my first PB&B, Aunt Sarah took my plate into the kitchen and returned with an apple pie. "Here you go," she said, passing it to me.

I honestly didn't make the connection between my errand to Ms. Mary's and the pie. "Wow, thank you, Aunt Sarah," I said, waiting for her to hand me a fork.

"That's for Ms. Mary, honey."

"Oh," I said.

"She'll be surprised, so just tell her it's a late birthday present."

The bottom of the dish felt warm in my hands. I tried to comprehend the idea of giving away a whole fresh apple pie.

"You want me to take all of it over there?" I asked, just to be sure.

"I'll make you one later, don't worry," she said. "Now, run it on over there while it's still warm."

"Yes, ma'am."

I stepped into my sandy flip-flops and headed down the stairs with the pie. Once on the street, I began to feel a little self-conscious. Particularly after two grown-ups, a man and a woman riding bicycles, passed by.

"Nice pie," the woman said.

The man laughed.

Jerk.

It did make me think, though: How many boys my age do you see walking down the street at the beach carrying pies? Before I could think of a quick reply should I see anyone else, I heard a female voice behind me say, "Hey, Ran."

I stopped and turned around to see Heather. Of course, it had to be Heather. Of all the scenarios I had imagined for seeing her again, me carrying a pie down the street wasn't one of them. Unable to hide the pie anywhere but right in front of me, I said, "Hi, Heather." My heart began to race in my chest as she walked toward me in a black bikini bottom and a white, cut-off, smiley-face t-shirt.

She flashed her perfect-white-teeth smile at me and asked, "What are you doing?"

"Um, I'm taking a pie to a lady who lives in a trailer." That sounded ridiculous.

"You're what?"

"There's this lady," I tried to explain. "And she lives over there." I motioned with the pie in the general direction of the trailer. "And this is her pie."

"Why do you have her pie?"

"My aunt made it. It's her birthday."

"It's your aunt's birthday?"

"No, it's Ms. Mary's birthday."

"Who's Ms. Mary?"

"The lady in the trailer. But I don't know her."

"You don't know her, but you have her pie?"

"Right. And it's not really her birthday. So, it's a surprise."

She paused as she studied the hopeful look on my face. "Are you always this confusing to talk to?" she asked.

"No, not usually," I said, trying to sound more confident.

"Well, I'm going to be at King's for a while. Once you finish with the pie, why don't you come hang out?"

"Groovy, I'll be there," I said, feeling good about my choice of words. But of course, I had to ruin it. "Without the pie," I added.

She gave a slight chuckle, said, "I'll catch you later," and walked away down the street.

OK, that could've gone better. But at least I got my first post-kiss Heather conversation out of the way. And she still wanted to meet me at King's. Maybe we could get snow cones again, I thought laughing to myself. That's assuming Joni would sell them to us. Regardless, I put a smile on my face and floated on over to Ms. Mary's.

Parked beside the trailer next to the tall marsh grass was an old cream-colored Volkswagen Beetle. It looked just like Herbie, but without the stripes and number 53 stickers. I climbed two steps and knocked on the door, then backed down and admired Joey's bush trimming work. After a moment, Ms. Mary opened the door. She was fully dressed, thank goodness, wearing a pink skirt and a light-yellow sleeveless shirt. I hadn't taken much notice of her appearance when we met in the beauty parlor, but she looked about the same age as Aunt Sarah. Her straight brown hair was styled like a younger woman, though. Kind of like my mother's, but with short bangs covering her forehead.

"Well, hello!" she said.

"Hi. This is from my aunt Sarah," I said robotically, extending the pie toward her.

"Is that an apple pie?" she asked, with more excitement than I'd anticipated.

"Yes, ma'am. It's a surprise."

"Oh, my goodness! It certainly is! Well, bring it on inside." She stepped back and held the door open for me.

I hadn't expected to go inside the trailer, but I didn't know if I was allowed to say no. So, I walked up the steps through the door. I expected it to be dark and cave-like inside, but it wasn't. Sunlight filtered through little white curtains covering small rectangular windows on the sides and back of the trailer. I noticed the floor had the same kind of indoor/outdoor carpet that my friend Henry Evans had in his basement playroom. To my right was a narrow counter with a small, turquoise-colored cooking range and matching sink. And on the opposite end of the room sat a table surrounded by three cushioned benches.

"You can set that right here on the counter, hon," she said.

I placed the pie on the counter and stood there unsure what to do next. The door was still open, and Heather was waiting for me at King's. I could always make a break for it.

"Would you like a piece?" she asked, pointing to the pie. "I have ice cream."

"Um," I said, weighing my options. Why was Heather always competing with food? And losing. "Yes, ma'am," I said. I was learning a lot about my priorities when it came to girls.

"Wonderful! You can have a seat right over there."

I sat down at the table and watched her get two plates from her only kitchen cabinet. I couldn't help but notice the lack of a bed anywhere in the trailer. "So, you live here?" I asked, more as a comment than a question.

"I sure do."

"But where do you sleep?"

"You're sitting on my bed," she said. "That table moves and the bed folds out from those cushions."

Just curious, I lifted the corner of my cushion. But I didn't see a bed, just a wooden box. As I tried to understand why a grown-up would be living in a portable house smaller than my bedroom, Ms. Mary served our pie and ice cream. With a smile, she sat down across from me.

"You look just like your father did when he was your age," she said as she cut off a piece of pie with her fork.

I was about to do the same but stopped. The room began to feel even smaller. How could this random hairdresser lady living in a trailer at the beach know my dad?

"You know my dad?" I asked.

"Mmm, this pie is still warm," she said, enjoying her pie. "I used to know your dad. He was a few years younger than me, but we grew up in the same neighborhood and went to the same schools."

As I listened, I took my first bite of pie and ice cream. Anything Aunt Sarah made seemed to work like a mild sedative when you ate it. All my fears and concerns about Ms. Mary and her weird trailer faded away in a sensory blur of apples, cinnamon, and vanilla ice cream.

"So, you grew up in Columbia like me?" I asked.

"I did. But I haven't lived there in a long time."

I took another bite of pie and thought to myself for a moment. When Joey and I sat on the dunes across the creek and he asked me what my dad was like, I struggled to give an answer. But now with Ms. Mary, maybe I could get some help. "What was he like?" I asked her.

"Who, your dad?"

"Hm-mm."

"Well, let me think about that for a minute," she said, looking up at her ceiling. "I remember your dad being a happy kid. Always smiling and laughing."

"He was?" I asked, revealing my surprise at hearing it.

"Sure. I remember my mother saying once that if Tommy had a tail, it would be wagging all the time."

I began to wonder if we were talking about the same person. "You called him Tommy?" I asked.

"Sure. What do people call him now?"

"Just Tom, I guess."

"Oh, well that's just an age thing. Tom sounds more manly than Tommy, don't you think?"

"I guess," I said, staring blankly at the ice cream melting into my pie. Her impression of my dad wasn't anything I could repeat honestly from my own experience. So, unfortunately, I was back to the generic answer I gave Joey.

"How's your pie?" Ms. Mary asked.

I noticed she was almost finished. "It's good, thank you." I stuffed a large forkload of pie and ice cream in my mouth and let my eyes wander around the room.

"Your aunt Sarah is a good cook, isn't she?"

"Hm-mm," is all I could manage.

"How's your uncle Breland?"

I don't know why but hearing his name startled me. I swallowed hard and said, "Oh, he's fine."

"Is he talking to you?" she asked with a smile.

Her question made me realize she must know Uncle Breland well too. "Yes, ma'am. Kind of. We talked about sandspurs one time."

She chuckled and said, "That sounds about right."

Ms. Mary seemed nice, but I felt a sudden longing for the more kid-friendly confines of King's Funland. Not to mention my date with Heather. "Um, I've got to go meet somebody," I said. "Is it OK if I go now?"

"Oh, sure, honey," she said taking my plate. "But please come back and see me again, sometime, OK?"

"Yes, ma'am," I said standing up from the table.

"And tell your sweet aunt that I said thank you for the pie."

"I will."

As I headed to the door, I noticed an old black-and-white photograph, hanging in a wooden frame next to the door. A young woman and a small boy sat on the beach, and I wondered who they were.

SIXTEEN

Anticipation

When I was in third grade, most boys, including myself, were very attentive to major happenings in the world of sports. The World Series and the Super Bowl, of course, were the two annual headliners. The ABC TV network started broadcasting NFL football games on Monday nights that fall, not that I was allowed to stay up and watch them. But the biggest sporting event of the year came in the spring. It was billed as *The Fight of the Century.* Undefeated heavyweight boxing champion Joe Frazier battled undefeated former champ and draft dodger Muhammad Ali in New York City.

With the anticipation leading up to the fight, and all the arguments over who was going to win it, I found myself in a war of words with a kid named Lucas Brown. Lucas was firmly in the Frazier camp. I, on the other hand, was enamored with Muhammad Ali's flashy boxing style and loud mouth. I thought he was funny. At some point, the Donaldson twins caught wind of our debate and decided to intervene. Without asking Lucas or me, they began spreading the word of a boxing match between the two of us to settle things once and for all. In no time, our bout was the talk of the school. And just like the real fight, people took definite sides over who they thought would win. The Brown-Fox fight, as it was billed, was scheduled for the Monday afternoon the day of the Frazier-Ali fight at a small grassy park in our neighborhood.

Lucas and I, having bonded over the attention our friendly argument had brought us, walked to the park together after school. Ironically, rather than talk about the upcoming Frazier-Ali fight or our contest, we spent most of the walk discussing bugs. We were just nine at the time, after all. When we arrived, the Donaldson twins were waiting with their own boxing gloves for us to use and a small crowd of kids around them. As Lucas and I slipped the big, padded leather gloves on our hands, the kids formed a circle around us. Without any ceremony, one of the twins said, "OK, go at it."

I had never personally been in a fight before but had seen Muhammad Ali box on TV. So, lacking a better example, I began doing my best Ali impersonation. Lucas positioned both his gloves under his chin and watched, unblinking, as I danced backward in a circle around him to the delight of the kids watching. I jabbed at Lucas intermittently as I bounced on my toes, enjoying myself while the small crowd chanted my name. Taking my show to the next level, I stopped, shuffled my feet back and forth, just like Muhammad, and threw a jab aimed right at Lucas's nose. Before my glove reached its target, Lucas threw his only punch of the fight. His glove sank deep into my stomach sending me to the grass in a folded, coughing heap. I never saw it coming.

When I stepped out of Ms. Mary's trailer door, I took one striding leap over the three wooden steps below. Before my feet could hit the ground, the singular focus of my day shifted to King's. With no more pies to deliver or food to tempt me, I felt free to set my mind on Heather. The way she looked at me with those big, blue, perfectly shaped eyes. The way her wet, orange-flavored lips felt on mine. The way she ate her snow cone. She was perfect. And she was waiting for me at King's. But first, I needed money.

I walked quickly back to the house to get a dollar. No, make that two dollars. Heather's worth it, I thought. I ran up the stairs, said "Hey" to Aunt Sarah as she rocked on the porch, passed along Ms. Mary's thank you for the pie as I ran into the den, grabbed my money from my room, and ran back down the stairs to the street. I smiled to myself all the way to King's. I couldn't wait to tell my mom that I was right about love. Maybe I should take Aunt Sarah's advice and write it in a letter.

As I neared the arcade I could see two boys, I'd say ten or eleven years old, bouncing on the outdoor trampolines. They faced each other from their adjacent mats and synced their bounces, going up and down together. Watching them as I turned onto the lane leading to the arcade, I witnessed something amazing. They counted their jumps out loud, one-two-three, and then bounced over to the other's trampoline, exchanging high-fives as they passed in the air. I couldn't help but laugh and clap as I went by. Maybe I could give that a try with Heather, I thought. Good thing I brought the extra dollar.

I stepped up to the arcade's wide entrance and glanced around before heading all the way in. It was as busy and noisy (in a good way) as I thought it would be, but I didn't see Heather anywhere. I thought perhaps she'd gone to the restroom, so I decided to just wait a few minutes. The barstool at the counter was available, but Joni wasn't in the order window. And without Joey around to beat in air hockey, I decided to just play a game of Skee-ball by myself while I waited.

I fed one of my dollar bills into the change machine, scooped the ten dimes into my shorts pocket, and stepped over to the first open lane. I have to say that my reason for playing Skee-ball had nothing to do with fun. Golfers might disagree, but rolling a ball into a hole was not, in and of itself, fun. My only use for Skee-ball was to score as many points as possible and walk away with a long string of prize tickets to trade in for free stuff. That was fun. And after rolling my first couple of balls into the forty-point hole I felt good about my chances. With my third ball in hand, Joni appeared at my side.

"Hey," she said.

I stopped my backswing and said, "Hey."

"When you finish your game, could I ask you for a favor?"

"Sure, what is it?"

"Just come see me when you're done."

If she were trying to distract me so I couldn't win enough tickets for a free snow cone, it worked perfectly. My last three balls went straight into the ten-point hole. I stared at the ticket slot waiting for at least one ticket to spit out. It didn't. Frustrated, I walked over to the counter. Joni was waiting in the order window.

"Can you come back here for a second?" she asked.

"Back there?"

"Yeah, just come around this way." She pointed me to the open doorway near the arcade entrance.

I followed her instructions and walked past yet another sign that said I wasn't supposed to be where I was going. After having ignored two trespassing signs with Joey, Joni had me walk past the *Employees Only* sign to find her standing beside a large table-top popcorn machine.

"Can you reach that box of cups up there?" she asked.

On top of the machine was a large cardboard box. I reached up and pushed the right corner toward me just a little, so the bottom was exposed, then did the same with the left. As I was about to pull the box toward me, I noticed a metal two-step stool under the back counter. "Could I use that to reach the box?" I asked Joni, pointing to the stool.

"Oh, sure," she said, seeming a little embarrassed.

She retrieved the step stool, and I used it to move the box off the popcorn machine to a table beside it.

"Anything else?" I asked.

"Um, no," she said, glancing around. "I guess that's it. Thank you."

I returned to my side of the counter, took a seat on the barstool by the order window, and looked for Heather. Joni leaned through the window on her elbows. Since it was just me for the moment, I asked her if I could get my snow cone.

"Sure, what flavor?" she asked.

"Orange, again," I said, smiling. As if I would ever order any other flavor.

"Oh, that reminds me," she said over her shoulder from the snow cone machine. But rather than finishing her thought, she topped off my snow cone, returned, and said, "Here you go. That's ten cents."

I placed a dime on the counter. "Reminds you of what?" I asked.

"Heather was here earlier," she said.

"Yeah, she told me to meet her here."

"She did?" she asked, lowering her eyebrows. "That's funny."

"Why is that funny?"

"Well, she just left with another boy."

"Are you sure?"

"Yep. They went out that way towards the beach."

I sat processing that in my head for a moment. That's the same way I went with Heather. But I was sure Joni was reading too much into it. "Maybe it was just her brother or something."

"She doesn't have a brother," Joni answered.

"Well," I said, without worry as I tried to think of another favorable explanation. "She'll probably be right back."

"I doubt it," she said.

"How come?"

"They were holding hands when they left."

Her words hit me like Lucas Brown's right hand to my stomach. I didn't see that coming. "I don't believe that," I said, feeling a little unbalanced on the barstool.

"I'm not tricking you," she said. "I promise."

My head was swimming; there had to be some mistake. "Well, I'm kind of her boyfriend," I said, hoping that was still true. "So, I don't think she would do that to me."

"Her boyfriend?" she asked as if she'd just heard something completely absurd.

"Yeah," I said, trying to assert some confidence.

"Since when?"

I sighed. It was like talking with Joey all over again. "Since the last time I met her here."

"Um, so you don't know Heather that well, huh?"

I was beginning to get a little annoyed. Despite Joni and Joey's skepticism, I knew what happened between us on the beach. "I know all I need to," I said, letting my irritation show a bit.

Joni shrugged and reached under the counter for a wiping cloth. "Well, she's off with Ronny, now," she said.

"Who is Ronny?" I asked.

"Just some local boy," she said. "Your snow cone is melting."

The orange syrup had dripped down the side of my cone and onto the counter without me noticing. "I'm sorry, can you just throw it away for me?" I asked, handing her the cone. Despite my defense of Heather, the thought of her with Ronny, whoever that was, had ruined my orange snow cone experience.

"You don't want it?"

"No, I think I'm done with orange snow cones for a while."

"Do you care if I eat it?" asked Joni, wrapping her cloth around the wet cone.

"Help yourself," I said. I sat there quietly while Joni ate my snow cone. I didn't know what to do, or say, or where to go.

"Do you like putt-putt golf?" asked Joni, crunching the orange ice in her mouth.

"Um, yeah, I guess," I answered half-heartedly. Putt-putt golf was the last thing on my mind. Where was Heather, and who the heck was Ronny?

"We should play sometime. It's free if you play with me."

Before I could respond to her invitation, I saw Heather walking back into the arcade from the beach entrance. Just ten minutes before, I would have jumped off my barstool and happily greeted her. But after talking with Joni, I just sat watching as she navigated her way around kids playing pool and air hockey on her way toward me. She had a smile on her face, but I assumed that Ronny had put it there. To my surprise, she waved as she got closer and said, "Hey, Ran!"

"Hey," I said, looking for evidence of orange syrup around her lips as she stepped up to me.

"Sorry, I missed you earlier," she said. "My cousin is here, and he wanted to go on the beach."

"Your cousin?" I asked, cutting my eyes at Joni. She shook her head at me as I turned my attention back to Heather.

"Yeah, anyway," Heather said, "I can't stay. I just wanted to say hey." She moved closer, pressing her body against mine.

I was about to say something, probably something stupid, when she slid her hand around my shoulder to the back of my neck and kissed me square on the lips.

She pulled away, smiled, and said, "Bye, sweetie."

"Bye," I said, my head floating like a balloon.

"I'll catch you later," she said, patting my knee as she turned to leave. "Bye, Joni!" she added with a wave.

I watched Heather until she disappeared out of the arcade. I was right, I thought to myself. I was definitely right. And with that thought, I turned to Joni. But she jumped to her own defense before I could say anything.

"I promise she was holding hands with Ronny. And he's not her cousin!"

"Uh-huh," I said, more confident than ever. "Joni, she just kissed me right in front of you."

"She just did that because I—" she stopped midsentence.

"Because you what?"

"I have to make popcorn," she said, quickly. "I'll see you later."

Joni left me sitting alone on the barstool, looking around the arcade. With a pocket full of dimes, I could've played more Skee-ball or some pinball. But replaying Heather's kiss in my mind was enough fun for me.

SEVENTEEN

Bridge Over Troubled Water

I had read through the part in *Where the Red Fern Grows* where Billy was summoned to his grandfather's house. He wasn't given a reason why his grandfather wanted to see him, but he assumed the worst. He spent the entire night before lying awake in bed worrying about the visit. As I walked back to the house from King's Funland, I could see Uncle Breland's truck parked in front of the house. The scene from the book floated through my mind, pushing thoughts of Heather aside. I didn't know what to expect when I got there, but with all that happened at the creek earlier, I could only assume the worst. Maybe Aunt Sarah would let me eat supper in my bedroom.

I made my way slowly up the steps of the house. My uncle was sitting on the front porch smoking a cigarette when I opened the screen door. "Hey, Uncle Breland," I said.

He put his cigarette in his mouth, tightened his lips around it, looked at me, and nodded. As he blew smoke from his nose, I assumed that was the end of our greeting and headed into the house to find Aunt Sarah. She was in the kitchen, of course, frying fish. The table was already set for three.

"Hey, Aunt Sarah," I said, happy to see her.

"Hello, honey," she said. "I talked to your mom a little while ago."

"You did? What did she say?"

"She was just checking on you. I told her you were being a good boy and minding your aunt and uncle."

"You didn't tell her I got sick in the fish, did you?"

"No, that's our little secret," she said with a smile. "We're going to be eating in just a minute, so why don't you go get washed up."

"Yes, ma'am," I said, heading into my room. I closed the door behind me, relishing a moment of privacy before sitting across the kitchen table from Uncle Breland. I didn't really see the need to "wash up," but knew Aunt Sarah was cooking right outside my door. So, in case she was listening, I turned on the water in my bathroom sink and let it splash around for a minute before turning it off. I looked at my reflection in the mirror and reminded myself to just say nothing about the creek. I wasn't sure which part he wanted to remain secret, but I resolved to just say nothing and eat.

"Ran, supper!" my aunt called from the kitchen.

I opened the door and saw Uncle Breland already sitting at the table. I took my seat across from him without making eye contact while Aunt Sarah prepared our plates.

"Did you and your friend have fun on the beach today?" she asked, placing a plate of fried fish, grits, and some little, round, fried green things in front of me.

"What are these?" I asked pointing to the mystery food.

"Those are fried okra," she said. "Try one."

Okra. It didn't sound like something you'd put in your mouth. Plus, I'd already thrown up once that day.

"Go ahead, I promise you'll like them," she said. "If not, you can give them to your uncle."

Again, giving my aunt the benefit of the doubt, I picked up an okra with my fingers and popped it in my mouth. I shouldn't have been surprised, but it was very good. I guess I didn't realize frying vegetables was a thing.

"Do you like it?" she asked.

"Yes, ma'am," I said, still crunching on the okra.

"Next time, use your fork," said Uncle Breland, sternly.

"Yes, sir," I said.

"So, tell me about your day on the beach," said Aunt Sarah, cutting off a piece of her fish and placing it in her mouth.

I looked at Uncle Breland, then back at Aunt Sarah. "Well, Joey and I walked to the south end," I said, hoping that would suffice.

"All the way to the creek?" she asked.

"Yes, ma'am," I said, cutting my eyes again to Uncle Breland.

"You didn't get in the creek, did you?" she asked, her fork hovering over her fish.

I was afraid she would ask that. And given Uncle Breland's warning not to tell anyone about him pulling me out of the water, I was torn about how to answer. But I didn't want to lie to my aunt Sarah's face. So, I braced myself and said, "Yes, ma'am."

"Honey, you promised not to do that. Do I need to call your mother and have her talk to you?"

"I told him it was OK," said Uncle Breland.

Aunt Sarah and I both turned our heads to my uncle.

"I was down there fishing," he said, "and I told him I would look after him."

"Breland," Aunt Sarah said, looking at him intently.

"It's OK, Sarah," he said. Uncle Breland looked at me and winked, then took a bite of his fish.

"Well," said Aunt Sarah, resetting herself. "I hope you had a good time."

"We did," I said, hoping that concluded my part of the conversation. I stuffed my mouth full of fish and grits and said, "Supper is really good."

"I'm glad you like it," said Aunt Sarah.

Uncle Breland looked at me and said, "Don't talk with your mouth full." I saw that faint, sandspur smile again hiding under his mustache.

I swallowed and said, "Yes, sir." And for the first time, I felt comfortable at their kitchen table.

EIGHTEEN

Keep On Truckin'

When I was growing up, we lived close enough to my elementary school that I could walk to and from school with ease. The only times my mom drove me were on rainy days. The temperature outside didn't matter. While she was fine with me freezing to death, she couldn't stand the thought of me getting wet. So, if it wasn't raining, I was walking. But after the bell rang one sunny afternoon in fifth grade, I bounced down the front steps of my school with Will Mason to find my dad sitting in the driver's seat of a shiny, yellow Triumph Spitfire convertible. The top was down, of course. And he was sporting a huge grin. I walked toward him with my mouth hanging open. It was like finding out that your mysterious, mostly absent dad was really James Bond the whole time.

Without telling anyone, including my mom, he had traded his 1968 Ford Galaxy 500 for the used 1970 Spitfire. Since it was only a couple of years old, it still looked brand new. He drove me home that day, which unfortunately only took three minutes. Still, with the wind in my hair and my arm resting on the door, I felt like a celebrity's kid for those three minutes.

With only two seats, the Triumph wasn't exactly a family car. And considering the fact that my dad only drove two miles back and forth to work, it sat undriven in our carport or behind his coffee shop most of the time. He would still give it a bath once a week and always had some reason to be outside tinkering with it when he was home.

I heard my mom tell someone on the phone that my dad wanted to get his midlife crisis out of the way early. I didn't know what that meant, exactly, but she thought it was funny. My dad's side of the story (or "excuse" as my mom put it) was that he wanted the Spitfire to be my first car when I was old enough to drive. He told me he was excited about teaching me how to work a stick-shift, and that I would have a cool car to drive to high school. But those plans evaporated six months after he bought it. A milk truck rear-ended him at a stop light and totaled the Triumph. Fortunately, my high school was also within walking distance of our house.

࿔

In what was becoming a habit, Uncle Breland knocked on my bedroom door before I was awake. "Time to get up, Turtle," he said.

Rather than having a conversation through the closed door, I said nothing and waited for him to open it.

"Time to get up, Turtle," he repeated, opening the door. "We need to be going."

Rolling over, I asked, "Going where?" I don't know why I bothered asking; I knew what he would say.

"You'll see," he said, right on cue.

"Can I eat first?"

"We won't be gone long. You can eat when you get back. Put some clothes on. I'll be on the porch."

"Where's Aunt Sarah?" I asked.

"She went to the store. Now, hurry up. Time's wasting."

He left my door open and exited the kitchen. What could possibly be so urgent, I wondered. Hopefully, it wasn't another overgrown lawn or dead fish emergency. Without knowing what I was in for, I hopped out of bed. I trudged through the den in the same clothes I slept in and made my way onto the porch.

Uncle Breland rose from his rocking chair and looked down at my bare feet. "You need something on your feet."

"Like shoes, you mean?" I asked, feeling like we'd done this before.

He sighed and nodded.

I left the porch to go look for my flip-flops. I searched my bathroom, my bedroom, and under my bed. Then under the kitchen table.

"Are these what you're looking for?" I heard Uncle Breland say from the porch.

Walking back to him, I found my flip-flops right beside the screen door where I'd stepped out of them the night before. "Yes, sir. Thank you," I said. "Sorry."

I followed him down the stairs and over to his pickup truck. "Where are we going?" I asked, walking to the passenger door.

"For a drive," he said.

He got in the truck and reached over to unlock my door. After a couple of tries, I was able to pull it open and climb up onto the vinyl bench seat.

Uncle Breland put his hands on the steering wheel, but he didn't start the truck. "Now," he said, turning to me, "I want you to watch everything I do over here. I'll talk you through it."

"Talk me through what?" I asked.

"How to drive a truck," he said, plainly.

I repeated what he said in my half-awake head to make sure I heard him correctly. Assuming that I had, I said, "But I'm twelve."

"Exactly," he said. "I learned to drive when I was your age. Now watch. I'm going to put the key in the ignition. But before I turn the engine over, I'm going to push the clutch pedal all the way down with my left foot."

"My dad used to have a yellow sports car with a clutch in it," I said.

"Yeah, I heard about that," he said, turning the key. "This truck has what they call 'three on the tree.' First, second, and third gear. Plus, reverse. The gear changer is right here on the steering column."

Before we backed away from the house, he showed me how to put the truck in each gear. I would pull the gear changer toward me and then down for first gear, push straight up for second, and pull straight down for third. Finding reverse was like first gear, but you pushed up instead of down.

"You got all that?" he asked.

"I think so," I said, still unsure what he was expecting of me, or why he was teaching me to drive his truck.

He backed onto the street, telling me what he was doing each step of the way. "Watch my feet," he said, as he shifted into first gear.

I watched him slowly lift his left foot off the clutch while he pushed down on the gas pedal with his right. We began to move forward slowly as he talked me through each gear. He drove us along the creek road all the way to the south-end parking lot, providing driving tips as we went. Some were obvious, like, "Always stop at stop signs." Some were strange, like, "If you see a squirrel in the road, don't try and guess which way he's going to run. Just drive straight and let him figure out how to get out of the way."

"How come?" I asked.

"That way, if he gets runned over, it's his fault, not yours."

I had to admit that made sense.

Once we reached the south-end parking lot, he drove the truck around the sandy loop and pointed it back the way we came. He put the gear shifter in neutral ("in the middle where you can wiggle it") and got out of the truck. I watched him walk around the back and open my door.

"Well?" he said, holding my door open.

I looked at him as if I had missed something, which I obviously had.

"Move over," he said, pushing me across the bench seat to the steering wheel. "You're gonna drive us home."

"Really?" I asked, as he hopped in the cab and shut the door.

"Just do everything I showed you. But remember, when you step on the brake, step on the clutch too. Got it?"

"Yes, sir," I said.

"All right, take us home," he said, settling in as a passenger.

I scooted myself closer to the steering wheel so I could reach the clutch pedal, then mashed it down as far as I could. Then I pulled the gear changer toward me and then down as far as it would go.

"OK, that's first gear," Uncle Breland confirmed. "Now what do you do?"

Without answering, I slowly let the clutch pedal rise under my foot while I pressed down gently on the gas. We started rolling forward. I was driving a truck! Sure, we were only going three miles an hour, but we were moving. And I was making it happen.

"Give it a little more gas," Uncle Breland said. "Let's get it up to about fifteen miles an hour."

That was five times faster than we were going, which scared me a little to think about. But, feeling brave, I got us up to ten miles an hour surprisingly quickly.

"OK, now put it in second," said Uncle Breland.

Since things were going so smoothly in first gear, I hated to make a change. But I took a deep breath, pushed down on the clutch, lifted the gear changer straight up, and eased back off the clutch. Just like that, we were in second gear going fifteen miles an hour.

The rest of the drive home was easy, except for turning. The steering wheel took all my strength to turn when we had to go right or left at stop signs, but I managed. Before we made our final left-hand turn toward the house, Uncle Breland told me to pull over and stop. We switched places again, and he drove us the rest of the way home. He parked the truck in its usual place in front of the house and turned it off.

"You did good, Turtle," he said.

"That was fun," I said. "Wait 'til I tell my mom I drove your truck!"

"Well, let's not do that just yet," he said.

"You want me to keep it a secret?"

"We don't want your folks worrying about you down here, do we?"

"No, I guess not," I said. "How about Aunt Sarah?"

"Why do you think I got you up while she was gone to the store?"

"So, she wouldn't know what we were doing?"

He nodded. "Let me talk with your aunt Sarah. But for now, keep this between us, OK?"

"Yes, sir," I said. I reached for the door handle but stopped. "Are we going to go driving again sometime?"

"Would you like that?"

"Yes, sir."

"OK then, here are the rules: You ask my permission before you go for a drive. You don't take anyone with you. You only drive when it's light out. And you don't leave the island. You think you can do all that?"

"You mean I can go driving by myself?"

"When I say it's OK, you can."

I thought about that for a second in worst-case scenario terms, like getting pulled over for going too slow or running over a squirrel. "What about police?" I asked.

"There are no police on the island. There's only the county sheriff, and he never comes over here. But don't leave the island. Got it?" He offered his hand to me.

"Got it," I said, shaking on it.

NINETEEN

Paper Roses

Despite starting my day with another first – driving a truck – I sat on the porch feeling a little frustrated. It was noon on Saturday, and I was sitting in a rocking chair by myself eating a sandwich made with leftover fried fish. Don't get me wrong, the sandwich was great; that wasn't the problem. It was Saturday. Before being forced to spend a summer in a beach house with no working television, I used to watch quality entertainment while I ate leftover food for lunch on Saturdays. For example, The Monkees' TV show used to come on every Saturday at noon. I never missed it. They stopped showing it around the time I turned eleven, replacing it with The Archies. The Archies were OK, but they weren't The Monkees. They weren't even real people. How can cartoon characters play musical instruments? And don't get me started about The Monkees not playing their own instruments. Maybe Davy Jones couldn't play the piano, but he did play a mean tambourine.

One of my favorite Monkees episodes had the band playing checkers on the beach when they were discovered by a big Hollywood movie producer. Thinking they were typical teenagers, he cast all four Monkees as extras in his next beach party movie starring some blonde, jerky, teen idol-type guy. But when the teen idol guy quit the movie, Davy got to play the main part. Then he turned into a jerk too.

Sitting there on the porch, replaying that episode in my head, I tried to imagine what it would be like to be a teen idol-type guy. Hanging out on the beach with girls in bikinis who tossed beach balls around and giggled for no apparent reason. And I wondered if I would be a jerk too. It seemed to go with the territory.

After lunch, I decided to walk down to the beach and look for Heather. I was no teen idol, but I did just learn to drive a truck. Maybe she would be impressed. I asked Aunt Sarah to send Joey my way if he stopped by, and then I headed down the stairs.

Once over the dunes and on the beach, there seemed to be a lot more people than I'd seen out there before. After a moment of taking in the scene, hoping to see the most beautiful thirteen-year-old girl ever, I realized why it seemed so crowded. The tide was more than halfway up the beach and people were scrunched up toward the dunes. I began to walk north along the waterline. But with everyone's chairs and towels so close together, I felt a little conspicuous scanning every group on the beach looking for Heather. I decided to play it cool and just walk along like I wasn't looking for her. Then, if she saw me, I could act all surprised. It was a good plan. But after walking halfway to the north end without hearing Heather call my name, I gave up and headed back toward King's.

It took me a few minutes to find the right spot in the dunes to cross over to King's. But I finally saw the arcade's low metal roof peeking up behind the dunes and made my way off the beach. Once inside, I immediately spotted Heather playing pinball. Standing next to her machine was a tall, tanned, blonde-haired, older boy. I assumed he was her cousin. Walking up with a smile, I said, "Hey, Heather!"

"Oh, hey," she said, barely taking her attention off her game.

The older boy stood on the other side of the machine looking at me as if I had something on my face.

"Whatcha doing?" I asked Heather.

"What does it look like?" she said, pressing her flippers and bumping the machine with her hip.

"Who's the kid?" asked the older boy.

"It's nobody," said Heather. Her face hovered over the glass as she watched her ball bounce around the table.

I may have been a little slow to read into the situation, but I was beginning to get the impression I wasn't welcome.

Pointing across the machine at the boy, I asked, "Who's this, Heather?"

"I'm Ronny," said the boy. "Who are you?"

"You're Heather's cousin?" I asked, hopefully.

Ronny let out a laugh and said, "Hardly, dude. Is there something you want?"

"I'm Ran," I said. Then, in an octave lower, I added, "I'm Heather's boyfriend."

He laughed louder and turned to Heather. "Seriously, Heather, who is this kid?"

Heather ignored both of us, as if we weren't there, while she focused on her game.

"Heather, what's going on?" I asked, trying to get her attention.

"I'm kind of busy right now," she said, pulling the ball shooter out and letting it go. "Why don't you go hang out with your little guardian angel over there?"

"What does that mean?" I asked.

"Just tell your friend Joni that I do what I want, with whoever I want." She finally looked at me and added, "Catch my drift?"

"What does Joni have to do with anything?" I asked, still confused.

"Hey man, why don't you book it?" said the boy. "We're trying to hang out here."

I wasn't ready to give up. "Heather—"

"Oh, look!" she shouted. "I just got bonus points!" She squealed and gave Ronny a hug around his neck.

I was suddenly invisible. I staggered back a few steps, then spotted Joni at the snack bar. I left Heather and Ronny behind and walked across the arcade to the order window. I may have run over there, I'm not sure. Let's just say I "moved swiftly across the arcade floor."

"Hey, Ran," said Joni, with a smile.

I jumped right to the point. "What's going on with you and Heather?" I asked. She was taken aback by my less-than-casual demeanor, but I couldn't hide my immediate need to understand what just happened.

"What do you mean?" she asked, looking a bit uneasy.

"She just told me to get lost and called you my guardian angel. What's that supposed to mean?"

"Ran, I–"

Interrupting, I added, "And she said to tell you she can do whatever she wants. Or something like that. What is she talking about?"

There was a momentary pause. Her eyes seemed to be searching mine for an answer. "Um…" she began.

"Yeah?" I asked, waiting.

"When you came in looking for her the other day," she began, "before you got here, I talked with her."

"OK, so?"

"Ran, you seem like a nice boy, and I…"

"What did you say to her?"

"You don't know Heather. I see how she treats boys and…"

"What did you say?"

"I was just trying to help you."

"What did you say?"

She paused, then said, "I told her to stay away from you."

"What!?" I said, recoiling from the order window.

"I was trying to save you from–"

"I don't need you to save me!" I shouted. And I left.

TWENTY

Love Hurts

Before I got to the beach, love was a simple concept to me. The way I understood it, by way of authorities like Stevie Wonder, Marvin Gaye, The Spinners, Cornelius Brothers & Sister Rose, Seals and Crofts, and of course Olivia, you lay eyes on that special someone and you're drawn to them like a magnet. Then you meet them, and suddenly you can't think of anyone else. All you want to do is be with them. Then there's that magical moment when fireworks go off and then... Well, they never really sing about what happens next, but I assumed you got married and lived happily ever after. With Heather, I had the magnet, the longing, and the fireworks. But what Marvin, Stevie, and the others never prepared me for was unwanted interference by a twelve-year-old girl named Joni.

When I got back to the beach house, I went straight to my room, shut the door, and threw myself on my bed. My aunt came to my door, without opening it, and asked if I was OK. I assured her I was and buried my face in my pillow. I wanted to go home. I thought about calling my mom and tried to imagine how that conversation might go. It didn't go well, even in my own mind.

I rolled over and watched the ceiling fan whirl around above me. The air felt good on my wet face. The thought that bubbled up inside my head, as I lay there, surprised me: I wished I could talk to my dad. Not about going home, but about girl stuff. I felt like I'd been thrown into a high school-level algebra class with no tutor, no textbook, and a teacher who only spoke Russian. I was lost. Joey always bragged about how his dad helped him understand things. I needed help too.

I opened my bedroom door and found Aunt Sarah in the kitchen. She was boiling something and stirring it with a long wooden spoon. "Hey, Aunt Sarah," I said. "Can I call my dad?"

"Your dad's at work this time of day, isn't he, honey?" she asked.

"Yes, ma'am. But I was kind of hoping I could talk to him about something."

"Is it anything your uncle or I can help you with?" she asked, still stirring.

I needed a man's advice, but the only topics on the table with Uncle Breland were yardwork, dead fish, and trucks. Girls did not exist. "No, ma'am," I answered. "I promise I won't be long."

"Well, all right," she said, seeming hesitant. "You wouldn't happen to know the number at the café, would you?"

"Um, no ma'am."

"Well, let me see if I have it in my address book." She pulled out a drawer from under the telephone table, retrieved a blue notebook, and flipped through it. "I do have it," she said. "Let me see." She began the rotary dialing process, which seemed to take forever. When she finished, she held the handset to her ear. "Here you go," she said, handing it to me. "It's ringing."

I heard my dad answer the phone in his official café owner voice. "Dad?" I said. "It's me, Ran."

"Hey, sport! How's the beach?"

"It's fine."

"Did you get my letter?" he asked.

"Yes, sir."

"We had the same teacher! How about that?"

"Yeah, that's weird," I said, ready to move on to my reason for calling. "Dad, I was wondering if–"

"Oh, hang on just one sec, Ran," he said. "No. Put it over there. No, on the counter. Thanks. It was supposed to be here last week. OK, sorry, what did you need, Son?"

"I was just hoping I could–"

"Hang on, Ran. I'm sorry, what? No, he was in earlier. He did. All right, good to see you too. Thank you. I'm sorry about that Ran. Go ahead."

"I just—"

"Susan, can you make that for me? I'm on the phone with my son. I'll be just a minute. OK, I'm here, Ran. What do you need?"

At that point, I gave up. "I just wanted to say hey, Dad."

"OK. Well, I'm so glad you called! Tell that big brother of mine I said, hello!"

"I will. Bye, Dad." I placed the handset back on the base.

Aunt Sarah stepped toward me from the kitchen. "Was he busy?" she asked, wiping her hands in her apron.

"Yes, ma'am," I said, my eyes down.

I didn't know why, but Aunt Sarah put her arms around me and hugged me.

"I'm making chicken pot pie for supper," she said, letting me go and straightening my shirt. "Does that sound good?"

"Yes, ma'am."

"It'll be ready in a little while."

๛

Supper was quiet. Between the secrets I had to keep with Uncle Breland and my lack of interest in talking about girls with either of them, I didn't have much to say. They talked to each other some, but I wasn't listening.

After supper, I retreated into my room and closed the door. I picked up *Where the Red Fern Grows* and found my folded page corner at the part where Billy was getting his dogs ready for the big coon hunting championship. I was sure they were going to win. After all, why would anyone write a whole book about two dogs who lost a raccoon hunting contest? But reading it kept my mind off other things. It did make me miss Pepper, though. My life seemed so much simpler before I came to the beach.

"Ran," my aunt Sarah called, "your friend Joey is in front of the house asking for you."

I left my room and went out on the porch. Joey was on his bicycle in the middle of the street. It was going to be getting dark soon, so I was surprised to see him. "Hey, what's up?" I said from the porch.

"Can you come down?" he asked.

I turned to my aunt. "Is that, OK, Aunt Sarah?"

"Sure," she said. "Don't be gone long, though."

"Yes, ma'am." I walked down the stairs in my bare feet and met Joey on the street. He hopped off his bike and steered it beside him as we started to walk.

"So, how's it going?" he asked.

"Fine," I said, lying.

"How about Heather?" asked Joey.

I gave him a look, wondering what prompted that specific question. "I don't want to talk about it."

"I thought you might say that."

"Why?" I asked, my defenses going up.

"I heard what happened at King's."

"How?" I asked, feeling slightly violated. "Did Joni tell you?"

"No, I heard it from Ronny Carter."

"Ronny?! You're friends with that jerk?"

"No!" he said, waving his hand. "He was in the store this afternoon with some other boys, and he was talking about it."

"Oh," I said. It felt strange being the subject of gossip so far away from home. I was offended and flattered all at the same time. "What were they saying?"

"Don't worry about it," said Joey. "I just wanted to make sure you were OK."

"I'd be a lot better if it weren't for Joni."

"What does Joni have to do with Heather?"

"She told Heather to stay away from me."

"Heather told you that?"

"No, Joni admitted it after Heather told me to get lost. Joni's why Heather was with Ronny."

"No," Joey said chuckling, "Heather was with Ronny because girls like Ronny the same way boys like Heather."

"Huh?" I tried to follow that but failed.

"Look, it sounds like Joni was just looking out for you, man. You should be thanking her."

"Are you crazy? Heather was..." I tried to think of a word better than "amazing."

"Heather was messing with you, dude. And Joni knew that. I tried to warn you."

"No, you just said Heather was different," I said. "That could mean anything." Joey didn't argue my point on that. "Why'd you even introduce me to her?" I asked, frustrated with the whole situation.

"You seemed desperate for a girlfriend," he said with a shrug. "I was trying to help you out."

"Well, thanks for nothing," I said, still irritated.

Joey laughed and said, "My dad always says—"

"And stop with the dad stuff!" I yelled out of frustration. "I'm so sick of hearing how great your dad is all the time!"

That wiped the smile right off Joey's face. Before I could collect myself and apologize, he got on his bike and rode away. I called after him, but he didn't even turn his head.

So, if you're keeping track, I lost Heather, Joni, and Joey all in one day.

TWENTY-ONE

I Can See Clearly Now

I'll be honest. When I was a kid, strategy board games were never my thing. I preferred fast-moving games of chance that had the appearance of strategy but took a lot less thought. Monopoly and Life took way too long to play, and I had no interest in buying hotels or acquiring children. On the other hand, a new game came out just a few months before I was sent to the beach called Connect Four. It was like vertical Tic Tac Toe. You could play as fast as you wanted, and when it was over, it dumped all the checkers out on the table in a big, noisy mess. I loved it.

Unfortunately, my friend Will Mason liked to play chess, the ultimate strategy game. His dad was teaching him how to play, and whenever I went over to their house, Will would challenge me to a game. My chess strategy was very similar to my initial approach to foosball. Rapid, random movements with quick, unpredictable results. That doesn't work very well in chess. The night of his end-of-the-year sleepover, Will beat me in three moves. Twice. And whenever he would win, which was every time, he would point his finger at me and shout, "Checkmate!" I would like to see Will play Joey in foosball.

Nearing the house from my aborted walk with Joey, I could see my aunt and uncle up on the porch. Aunt Sarah was rocking back and forth while Uncle Breland sat unmoving. Given the kind of day I'd had, my first thought was to say hello as I passed through the porch quickly then lock myself in my room. But as

I climbed the stairs and opened the screen door, I was drawn to the empty chair next to Aunt Sarah. I took a seat and began rocking along with her. I just wasn't ready to be alone.

"How was Joey this evening?" she asked.

"Oh, he's fine," I said, not wanting to get into it.

"He sure was in a hurry when he rode by a minute ago," she said, glancing my way.

"Yeah, he, um…had to get home," I said, improvising.

Aunt Sarah and I rocked quietly for a few minutes, while Uncle Breland just stared ahead into the dusky sky. He wasn't smoking, which I was thankful for. Aunt Sarah finally broke the silence.

"You know, Ran, when I was a little girl, my family used to vacation in this very house."

"Really?" I said, surprised. "It's that old?"

"Yes, it is," she said, laughing. "My grandfather built this house a long time ago."

"Wow," I said. "I didn't know that."

"Hm-mm. I remember one summer, when I was just a little older than you, my friend Fran Reynolds from Andrews and I were sitting on our towels out on the beach. And these two boys that she knew came up to talk to us. And one of them…" She paused as she smiled. "One of them was the most handsome boy I'd ever laid eyes on. His name was Rory. We hit it off the moment he sat down next to me. We spent the rest of that day talking and laughing and swimming. I was in heaven. I just thought Rory was the cat's meow."

"And then what happened?" I asked.

"Nothing," she said. "I never saw him again."

I sat looking at her. There had to be more to the story than that. "That's it?" I asked. "That's the end?"

"Hm-mm," she said, her eyes on mine as if she were expecting something.

I sat there for a moment wondering why she told me all that. Was it just Aunt Sarah rambling on about her childhood? Or was she trying to tell me something? The loose parallel with Heather seemed more than coincidental, but I hadn't shared anything about that with Aunt Sarah. How could she know? She had proven her powers of deduction before, but if my suspicion was correct, this was on the level of *Columbo*, not *Scooby Doo*.

I looked past Aunt Sarah to see Uncle Breland's eyes on me. He nodded slightly, then turned his gaze back toward the ocean.

"I'm going to have some ice cream," said Aunt Sarah. "Would you like some, Ran?"

"Yes, ma'am," I said, by default. Who would ever say no to ice cream?

"I'll get you a bowl. Would you like some too, Breland?"

"No, thanks."

While Aunt Sarah was getting my ice cream, I sat there alone with Uncle Breland. Despite our truck driving adventure, awkward silence remained our normal mode for spending time together. But finally, without turning his head, he said, "Your aunt Sarah is a wise woman."

"Yes, sir," I answered, curious to see if more insight was coming. But he said nothing else.

Aunt Sarah returned with our bowls of vanilla ice cream. We ate them there on the porch without saying much of anything. After I finished, I sat with the empty bowl on my lap and listened to the cicadas sing. If nothing else, all my angst over Heather, Joni, and Joey faded away for just a moment. It's amazing what a good bowl of ice cream can do.

As I sat there, I thought more about Aunt Sarah's story. And I looked for the wisdom Uncle Breland suggested was hiding in it. As I understood it, she experienced something special with someone for a day, and then it was over. Forever. And she seemed fine with it. That was a hard lesson for a rising seventh grader to absorb. But I wanted to believe she had a reason for sharing that with me.

"Aunt Sarah," I said, "weren't you sad that you didn't see Rory again?"

"I was for a little while. Very much so. But then I let it go."

"Why? I mean, if you really liked him, why'd you give up?"

"Honey, just because you lose someone, that doesn't mean you lose your hopes and dreams. Those are yours. No one can take them away from you."

I thought about that for a minute, trying to translate it into something practical. "You mean," I said, "just because you meet the perfect person, and things are going great, you shouldn't let it bother you if someone sticks their nose in where it doesn't belong and ruins it forever?"

Aunt Sarah smiled. "Well, that sounds pretty specific," she said. "Did something like that happen to you?"

"Yes, ma'am."

"What's the perfect girl's name?"

"Heather."

"And did Joey do something that messed things up for you and Heather?"

"No, ma'am. Joni did. She works at King's. And she told Heather to stay away from me."

"Oh. I see. Why do you think she did that?"

"She said she was trying to help me or save me from something. Like Heather was bad."

"Hmm. So, why did Joey come to see you tonight?"

"He heard what happened and wanted to see if I was OK."

"That was nice of him, don't you think?"

"Yes, ma'am."

"And what does Joey think about Heather?"

"He agrees with Joni. That she was looking out for me."

"I'm guessing you didn't want to hear that, did you?"

"No ma'am."

"So, out of Heather, Joni, and Joey, who treats you more like a friend?"

"What do you mean?"

"I mean, out of those three, who is looking out for you and concerned about you?"

"Well, Joni and Joey, I guess."

"OK, then," she said as if she'd proved something.

"But that's different," I argued. "Heather was my girlfriend, not my friend."

"Ran, maybe that's what Joey and Joni were trying to tell you," she said, with a knowing look. She might as well have said checkmate.

I lowered my head in defeat and said, "I think I see what you mean."

"I told you," said Uncle Breland.

"But, Aunt Sarah, did you know already about Heather when you told me your story?"

"No, honey," she said, "but I had a feeling you were having girl trouble."

"It was that obvious?" I asked, a little embarrassed.

"We've got a few years on you, Turtle," said Uncle Breland.

"Your uncle and I are always here for you, Ran," she said with a pat on my knee.

I was surprised at how good that made me feel. "Thank you, ma'am," I said. On that note, I decided to call it a day and head to my room. I stood up with my empty ice cream bowl. "Can I take your bowl for you, Aunt Sarah?" I asked.

"Oh, well, thank you, Ran," she said, surprised.

I took our bowls into the kitchen, rinsed them in the sink, and put them in the dishwasher. Returning to the porch, I had one more question. "Hey, Uncle Breland, what time does the sun come up in the morning?"

"Around six, I guess. Why?"

"Are you up then?"

"I can be."

"Would you wake me up a few minutes before six tomorrow?"

"I'll knock on your door at 5:45."

"That's perfect. Thank you, sir. Goodnight."

"Goodnight, Turtle."

TWENTY-TWO

Here Comes the Sun

The knock on my door startled me. But Uncle Breland did what I had asked him to do. A quick look out my bedroom window told me it was still dark outside, but the sky over the ocean seemed lighter. Skipping my usual ten minutes of sleepy lounging before getting out of bed, I hopped up and turned on the overhead light. While I had slept in my clothes again, I decided to put on something fresh. After a minute of sorting through my wardrobe on the floor to find what might be considered clean, I settled on a red Honda Motorcycle t-shirt and some cut-off jeans. I even brushed my teeth before I left my room. Uncle Breland was already sitting in a rocking chair smoking a cigarette when I stepped out on the porch.

"Where you headed this morning, Turtle?" he asked.

"I'm going down on the beach and watch the sun come up," I said, feeling a little grown-up for saying that.

He put his cigarette in his mouth and nodded. I'd learned that was my uncle's way of ending conversations. Much like my grunts, just more effective.

I headed down the stairs in my bare feet and started off toward the beach. Trying to avoid sandspurs lurking beside the road, I walked on the rough pavement, which made me wish I'd worn my flip-flops. There was just no right answer when it came to footwear at the beach.

Walking up the access path toward the dunes before six in the morning felt a bit weird. The air was completely still. No one was around. And the only sound came from the occasional slap of a wave breaking. I felt like the only person awake on the island, besides Uncle Breland. Once I reached the top of the dunes I stopped and looked around for Joni. The tide was out, so the beach was wide, flat, and empty. The only life I could see in either direction was a black Lab, up the beach to my left, digging a hole while his owner egged him on. Not knowing where Joni liked to watch the sunrise, I decided to head north toward the dog. If nothing else, I might get to play with it, if the man would let me.

The beach was getting brighter quickly. A light glow of orange was starting to appear just above the horizon. I wanted to find Joni before the sun came up so I could watch it with her if she'd let me. I hurried my pace and passed the dog without stopping to say hello. To my left, I could see the roof of King's over the dunes. And there, right in the spot where Heather and I had kissed, sat Joni, patiently waiting for the sunrise.

Her eyes were on the ocean, so I didn't know if she had seen me approaching. Even when I was just a few feet away, she still hadn't turned her head toward me.

"Hey," I said, stepping closer.

"Hey," she said without looking at me.

OK, she obviously knew it was me, which meant she wasn't looking at me on purpose. That was a bad sign. But I couldn't just turn around and leave. There was no quick exit from the beach. So, I stuck to the plan. "Can I watch with you?" I asked, still standing.

"Sure," she said as she watched the black Lab chase a tennis ball down the beach in front of us.

I sat down on the sand next to her, but certainly not as close as Heather did with me. I was where I wanted to be but had no idea what to say.

"This is going to be a good one," said Joni, letting me off the hook for a conversation starter.

"How can you tell?" I asked.

"See those clouds just above the water? They're gonna light up in a minute like they're on fire."

That sounded great, but I really needed to fix things with her before I could enjoy the sunrise. "Um, I need to thank you," I said.

"For what?" she asked.

"For saving me."

"Oh. You already thanked me for that."

"No, I mean Heather. That's the second time you've saved me."

She finally turned her head to me and said, "I thought you didn't need saving."

"Turns out I was wrong about that."

"Well, you're welcome," she said, pushing the sand with her bare feet. "What changed your mind?"

"I talked with Joey," I said. "And my aunt. They both said you were looking out for me."

"Oh. Joey's nice. And tell your aunt I said thank you."

"I will."

"Oh, look," she said, pointing to the horizon.

While we'd been talking, the few low clouds began to glow bright yellow against a deep orange sky.

"Here it comes," she said.

The top edge of the yellow sun crept over the dark water, moving upward much quicker than I expected. I turned to look at Joni. The sunrise was beautiful, but the look on her face as she watched was even more so. "You like this, don't you?" I asked.

"It's my favorite thing," she said, her eyes moving around the sky.

"I can tell," I said, smiling.

She glanced at me and blushed.

We sat there quietly for a minute, watching the Lab retrieve the tennis ball from the waves.

"So," Joni started, "you don't think it's weird to come out here and watch it?"

"Not at all," I said. Her question made me think about Joey. "I think I owe Joey an apology too, by the way."

"Why?"

"Well, when he and I were talking about everything last night, I was a little frustrated."

"Yeah, I know," she said, smiling.

"Yeah, sorry. And Joey's always talking about his dad, you know? My dad this, my dad that. It's really annoying. And I kind of told him I was tired of hearing about how great his dad is."

"You said that to him?" she asked, seeming a bit alarmed.

"Pretty much."

"What did Joey do?"

"He just got on his bike and rode away," I said. Joni stayed quiet, but I could tell she was troubled. "What's wrong?" I asked.

She looked at me and said, "Joey's dad never came back from Vietnam."

"Vietnam? Like the war in Vietnam?"

"Hm-mm."

That didn't make any sense to me. "Are you sure about that?" I asked. "Joey talks about him like he's here."

"I know. I think he's having a hard time with it. I guess he's hoping his dad might still come home someday."

"Oh, my gosh," I said, shaking my head. "I feel terrible. And now I don't know when I'll see him again."

We sat thinking for a minute. "You could always go to the store when he's working," suggested Joni.

"That's an idea," I said. "I'll see if my aunt can take me after she gets home from church."

"Let me know how it goes," she said. She began to stand up. "I should get back now. My mom's making breakfast."

I got up and brushed the sand off my shorts. "Thanks for letting me watch with you."

"Anytime," she said. "Come see me later?"

"Sure," I said. "No orange snow cones, though."

"We'll try something different this time," she said with a smile.

TWENTY-THREE

Sundown

After watching the sunrise with Joni, I went back to the house and took a nap. That was after eating a quick bowl of the Captain, of course. Without worrying about Uncle Breland banging on my door, I managed to sleep until almost lunchtime. Aunt Sarah had just come home from church when I woke up and offered to make me a sandwich with some leftover meatloaf she found in the freezer the day before. Like the PB&B and the okra, my initial skepticism proved unnecessary. She warmed the meatloaf in the oven, put a thick ketchup-soaked slice between two pieces of bread, and served it with Pringles. Her winning streak continued.

After lunch, I went down to King's to see Joni and maybe find Joey. But an older girl was working instead of Joni. I asked about her, and the girl said she'd be working later. Joey wasn't around either, so I started toward the exit when I heard, "Hey look, it's Heather's boyfriend," followed by some hearty, teenage boy laughter.

I turned around to see Ronny Carter and two other boys. If they hadn't been standing beside the air hockey table, I probably would have just kept walking out the door. But instead, I headed straight toward them. "Hey, Ronny," I said.

"Hey, kid," he said. "Looking for your girl?" The other boys enjoyed that.

"No, I was hoping to play some air hockey. You wanna play?"

"Are you sure?" asked Ronny, almost laughing.

"I'll pay for the first game, loser pays after that," I said, repeating Joey's offer. "Deal?"

"You're on," said Ronny.

I slipped fifty cents in the slot and woke up the table. We grabbed our pushers and started play. He scored a quick goal before I even knew what had happened.

"One-zip!" he said, high-fiving his buddies.

I evened things up a few seconds later. That's when Heather walked in. Ronny held the puck with his pusher to stop play as she approached the table.

"Hey, babe," he said to Heather.

Her eyes bounced back and forth between Ronny and me. "How did *this* happen?" she asked.

"Just having a little fun with the kid, here," he said. He turned to me and asked, "You ready?"

"Yep," I said, more determined than ever.

The puck ricocheted around the white surface for a few seconds before disappearing into Ronny's goal.

"Two-one," I said.

The sequence repeated.

"Three-one," I said.

The smiles were gone from Ronny and his friends' faces.

The table had a time limit, so the air stopped blowing with me winning 6-1. "Want to play again?" I asked Ronny.

"Nah," he said. "Heather's here, so we're gonna hang out."

"You're just going to let him beat you like that?" Heather asked. "Play him again."

Ronny looked at the grin on my face, then bummed some change from one of his friends. We played again, and he lost 5-2.

"Well, I've gotta skitty," I said, trying to suppress my joy. "Thanks for the game, Ronny. You guys have fun."

I laughed to myself all the way back to the house. I couldn't wait to tell Joey.

The afternoon passed by rather quickly. Aunt Sarah drove me to the store to see if Joey was working, but they said he didn't come in. So, once back at the house, I just settled in and read my book. Uncle Breland had gone somewhere, and Aunt Sarah kept me company on the porch. I decided against going back to King's. I didn't think anything could top beating Ronny, so I just stayed at the house. After supper, Aunt Sarah and Uncle Breland had to go visit someone they knew at the hospital in Georgetown.

"Watch the house," Uncle Breland said.

"You stay right here, Ran," said Aunt Sarah. "We'll be back after a while."

"Yes, ma'am," I said. Where else would I go, I thought. After all, the big coon hunting championship was about to get going. I had to see if Old Dan and Little Ann were going to win the big trophy.

It was kind of nice having the house to myself. Just feeling the breeze on the porch while the sky slowly faded from light orange to black was a nice way to end the day. After a little while, I happened to look up from my book and see Joni walking swiftly down the street in my direction. When she was still a house away, I shouted to her. "Joni!"

She looked up and saw me on the porch.

"Where are you going?" I asked.

"I'm coming to find you. Have you seen Joey today?"

"No. I went to the store, but he wasn't there. They said he didn't come in."

"Can you come down?" she asked.

I hopped up from my chair and jogged down the stairs to meet her in front of the house. "What's up?"

"Joey's mom just called the arcade looking for him. She doesn't know where he is. They got some news about his dad this morning, and she hasn't seen him since. She's been all over the island and can't find him anywhere. She sounds worried."

I'd only been a handful of places with Joey, but something he said when we were across the creek jumped into my mind. "I think I know where to look," I told Joni.

"Where?"

"You know those big dunes on the other side of the creek?"

"On DeBordieu?"

"Yeah, I think he's down there."

"That's a long way to walk without being sure."

I turned around and saw my uncle's truck still parked at the house. They had taken Aunt Sarah's car to the hospital.

"We'll take my uncle's truck. Want to come?"

"In the truck?"

"Yeah, I can drive."

"But you're twelve."

"I know," I said. "Hang on a sec." I ran up the stairs and into the den. Grabbing the truck keys from the hook above the phone, I ran back downstairs and said, "Come on."

Joni moved slowly toward the truck as I climbed in the driver's side. I leaned over across the seat and pushed the passenger door open. "Come on, get in."

"You're sure your uncle's OK with this?" she asked.

"He's not here right now. But he taught me."

Joni slowly climbed in and shut the door. "I don't know about this," she said.

"We'll be fine," I said. "Trust me."

I turned the ignition key without pushing down on the clutch, causing the truck to hop forward. "Sorry, about that," I said. My second try was successful.

"You need to turn your lights on," Joni said.

It took me a minute to figure out how to do that, but once they were on, I backed out onto the street and eased the truck into first gear. Despite us only going about ten miles an hour, Joni braced herself like she was waiting for that first big hill on a roller coaster at Myrtle Beach.

When we reached the south end, I parked and asked her to wait in the truck while I crossed over to the DeBordieu side of the creek to find Joey.

"No, I'm going to make sure you get to the other side first," she said, getting out of the truck with me.

"I think I learned my lesson," I said. "I'll be fine."

"Sorry, but I'm still going to watch you."

We walked down to the creek together. The tide was coming in, thank goodness, and the water was moving slowly. Getting across was easy. I looked back at Joni and waved before heading on toward the dunes. While it was dark, I could still see where Joey and I had gone before and began climbing up the face of the tall dune. About halfway up, I saw a silhouetted figure sitting on top.

"Joey!" I said, climbing toward him.

"Go away, Ran," he said without looking at me.

"Your mom is worried about you," I said, reaching the top. "She's got everyone looking for you."

"Why do you care?" he asked, glancing up at me.

"Because we're friends, man," I offered.

Joey didn't agree or disagree. He said nothing.

I took a seat on the sand next to him. "I'm sorry about what I said last night." I waited for a moment to see if he would accept my apology. He said nothing, so I tried again. "It sounds like you've got a great dad, Joey. Mine never has time for me, so I guess I was just jealous. I'm sorry. I didn't mean to upset you."

Joey remained silent, just staring off into the distance. I didn't know what else to say. I began to wonder if my being there was a mistake.

"Last year," he started, "we got a telegram saying that my dad was missing in action in Vietnam. It didn't say he was killed. Just missing. I knew he was still alive somewhere over there. He had to be." Joey paused for a moment, his eyes on the ocean before him. "About a month later," he continued, "my mom found out his unit came home without him. Then, just before school started, the man who used to be his commanding officer came to our house. My mom sent me to my room, so I didn't hear everything. But she told me he couldn't tell her anything about what happened, just that he was sorry."

"That was nice, I guess," I said. "To say he was sorry, I mean."

"He should be sorry. It's his fault. The war was practically over. Everyone was coming home. It was his job to keep my dad safe."

"How old was he? The officer guy."

"I don't know. Old, you know, forty-something maybe. You remember that house with the crab trap?"

"Yeah."

"That's his house."

"Oh," I said, rethinking our visit there.

"Then this morning we got another telegram. I found my mom crying in the kitchen with her head on the table. She couldn't even tell me what it said. So, I read it myself."

"What did it say?"

"It said they confirmed my dad was killed in action. They recovered his body, and they're sending him home to be buried."

"Joey, I'm sorry."

"After I read it, I just ran out. I shouldn't have done that. I shouldn't have left my mom like that. I just…" Joey paused, tightened his lips, and shook his head. "It's not fair, Ran. It's just not fair."

As I saw the tears streaming down Joey's face, all the things I'd been whining or worrying about since I got to the beach seemed so distant. I wished there was something I could say or do to fix things for Joey. But for the first time in my life, death had entered the picture. And I had no words for it. We sat there for a while, staring into the darkness without saying anything.

"I played Ronny in air hockey today," I finally said.

Joey wiped off his face. "Did you beat him?"

"Twice. Right in front of Heather."

Joey laughed. "I wish I had been there to see that."

"Me too."

"You know Ronny was one of the boys who suckered us into swimming down there," he said, pointing his thumb over his shoulder at the pond below.

"Well, you said you wanted payback."

"Yeah. I think we can call it even, now," said Joey.

Talking about King's reminded me that Joni was sitting in the truck, waiting. "Why don't you let me take you home."

"How?" asked Joey.

"I've got my uncle's truck."

"You drove his truck here?"

"Yeah, he taught me how to drive it."

"But you're twelve."

"I know. But it's right over there across the creek. Joni's in it too."

"Why is Joni with you?"

"She came to my house and told me your mom had called King's looking for you. I thought this might be where I'd find you."

"Thank you, man," he said, looking at me. "I'm glad you're here."

Joey and I swam back across the creek and got into the truck soaking wet. I hadn't thought about needing towels to sit on and hoped Uncle Breland wouldn't notice the wet seats. Joni sat in the middle and tried to make small talk on the way to Joey's house. I stayed quiet so I could focus on my driving. I kind of liked driving in the dark with the headlights on. It was like being in the *Adventures of Jonny Quest*. Think about it: A twelve-year-old boy operating heavy machinery on a night-time search and rescue mission. That was a whole episode, right there.

We crossed over the south causeway to the mainland side of the marsh and followed Joey's directions to his house. As we came to a stop at his mailbox, his mom opened their front door and stood waiting. He thanked us both, climbed out and closed the door. We watched Joey make his way toward the house and up the front steps. His mom wrapped her arms around him. They held each other in the open doorway without moving as I drove away.

Joni was surprisingly quiet on the way back to the house until I mentioned that I hoped my uncle was still gone when we got there.

"Why?" she asked. "Do you think he'll be mad you took his truck?"

"Well, I was just thinking of all the rules I had to follow if I wanted to drive it."

"What were they?"

"First, I had to ask him if it was OK."

"Nope," she said.

"It had to be daylight outside."

"Nope."

"I couldn't take anyone with me."

She giggled and said, "Nope."

"And there was one more."

"Did you have to stay on the island?" she asked.

"That's it. How'd you know?"

"There are never any police on the island."

"That's what Uncle Breland said." The reality of our little rescue trip began to sink in. "I broke every one of his rules."

Joni shook her head and said, "Your uncle's going to be so mad."

"Thanks," I said grimly.

"Sorry."

I came to the last stop sign before we reached the house and let the truck idle for a moment. "He's probably gonna lock me in a closet," I said.

"Why would he do that?"

"I don't know; he just scares me sometimes."

I turned left onto our street. Up ahead, in the glare of the headlights, stood Uncle Breland, smoking a cigarette in front of the house. "Oh, no, there he is," I said leaning over the steering wheel. "Oh, I'm in so much trouble."

I turned the truck into the same spot I took it from and turned off the ignition. Joni got out first. Uncle Breland stood facing her a few feet away. I hopped out and walked around to the front of the truck.

My uncle looked at Joni and said, "You can go home, little girl."

Joni looked straight at Uncle Breland. All in one breath she said, "Ran just rescued his friend Joey. That's why we took your truck. Joey's dad died in Vietnam, and he just found out and ran away. Well, not away-away, but he was missing. And his mom called the arcade because she was worried and was looking for him, so I came and got Ran and Ran knew where to look so we found him and took him home. So, please don't be mad at Ran. He's a hero."

Uncle Breland stood motionless, looking at Joni. "Are you through?" he asked.

"Yes, sir."

"You're Carlton's little girl, aren't you?"

"Yes, sir."

"You can run on home now."

Joni gave me a quick wave and began her walk down the street. Uncle Breland turned and looked at me. I braced myself for what was about to come.

"Can I have my keys?" he asked.

"Uncle Breland, I'm sorry I drove without asking. And that it was dark, and I had someone with me, and that I left the island."

"You left the island?"

"Yes sir. Joey lives across the marsh."

Uncle Breland put his cigarette between his lips. The end glowed bright orange for a couple of seconds, lighting up his face.

"I'm sorry, Uncle Breland, but it was kind of an emergency, and Joey was all the way down at the south end, so…"

He blew smoke from under his mustache and extended his hand toward me. "My keys?"

"Oh, sorry," I said, handing him the keys. I took a step back and stood at attention.

"How'd it drive in the dark?" he asked.

"Um, fine," I said, anxiously bracing myself for the worst.

He turned his attention toward the truck. "It's got a blinker light out," he said. "I need to get that fixed." He looked at me, then turned and started up the stairs, leaving me behind. "You coming inside?" he asked, plodding upward.

"Yes, sir," I said, snapping myself out of shock. I was still alive. And not in a closet.

TWENTY-FOUR

Help Me

I didn't see Joey again for two or three weeks. Aunt Sarah read in the Georgetown newspaper that his dad's body was going to be flown to the airport in Charleston, but the funeral would be at an old Episcopal church near Pawleys on the other side of Highway 17. Joni said a ghost named Alice haunted the cemetery over there. She said if you walked around Alice's grave six times and put a gift on her stone marker, she would grant you one wish. I asked Joni if she ever did that, but she hadn't. Her older sister had, though. She made a wish to meet David Cassidy. Which made me wonder if Alice might know Olivia.

On the 4th of July, my aunt Sara and I made homemade peach ice cream out on the front porch. She poured the fresh peaches and cream into a big metal container, closed the lid, and placed it in a wooden bucket. Then Uncle Breland poured ice and salt into the bucket all around the ice cream container. My job was to turn a handle, without stopping, to make the ice cream turn around and around inside the bucket. It was easy at first, but the thicker the ice cream got, the harder it was to turn. And sometimes the ice would get stuck between the bucket and the container, and the handle wouldn't turn at all. Uncle Breland would stab the ice with a screwdriver and say, "Keep turning, Turtle."

While I was making the ice cream, about six or seven cars and trucks, all decorated for the 4th, rode by the house with people blowing their horns and yelling *Happy 4th!* I asked Uncle Breland what that was about.

"It's supposed to be a parade," he said. "A few people started doing that on the 4th a few years ago."

"We should decorate your truck and drive around with them," I said.

He chuckled lightly. "Maybe next year. Keep turning."

That made me wonder where I would be the next Fourth of July. Would I be at the beach again? Or would I be at home? Where did I want to be? I was surprised to find I didn't know the answer to that question. The first few weeks at the beach were a little challenging. But since then, I'd started to feel more comfortable. Not that I didn't miss Pepper and TV and my own bed. But I wasn't scared of getting locked in a closet anymore. And the food was really good. And I enjoyed hanging out with Joni at the arcade. I'd even watched a couple more sunrises with her. But I learned not all sunrises were worth getting up for. The last one was cloudy and wasn't much to look at. But I watched it with Joni. And that was worth getting up for.

While Joey wasn't around, whenever I would go to King's I'd just sit on my barstool and keep Joni company in between customers. She finally moved the barstool around to her side of the counter so I could just sit beside her while she worked. That was fun until her dad found out. Joni said he was concerned about insurance or something like that. So, I moved back around and talked to her through the window. Sometimes I'd play Skee-ball. Other times I'd play pinball. Then I'd drift back over and talk to Joni. One afternoon I paid seventy-five cents to bounce on one of the trampolines outside for thirty minutes. It was a blast until Heather and Ronny walked by and laughed at me. It was the curse of being twelve. Kid things were still fun, but you weren't supposed to be seen enjoying them.

Joey finally stopped by the house one morning. I saw him walking down the street and went down to meet him.

"Hey, man!" I said, holding out my palm to give him five.

"Hey, what's up?" he said, slapping my hand.

"How'd everything go with your dad?"

"It was fine, I guess."

I leaned against Uncle Breland's truck and asked, "How's your mom doing?"

"Better," he said, a little unsure. "She's starting to get better." Joey paused for a second and looked down the street. "You know, the whole time my dad was gone, she never let me see her worried or upset, even after he was missing. But it's been different the past few weeks. She's been crying a lot."

"That stinks," I said, not knowing what else to say.

"Yeah," said Joey, looking down. "What have you been up to?"

"Not much," I said. "I've been reading a lot."

"For school or for fun?"

"For school. It's this book called *Where the Red Fern Grows*."

"We're supposed to be reading *To Kill a Mockingbird* this summer, but I haven't started it, yet. What's yours about?"

"It's about two dogs that win a raccoon hunting contest."

"That's it?" Joey asked.

"Pretty much."

"Wanna trade?" he asked, chuckling.

"No, thanks. Besides that, I've just been hanging out at King's."

"You seen Heather?"

"Just a couple of times. A few days ago, she and Ronny caught me jumping on the trampolines."

"What's wrong with that?"

"I don't know," I said, shrugging my shoulders. "It was just me out there bouncing, and they laughed at me."

"Who cares? Let 'em laugh. Trampolines are fun."

"I know; I just felt like a dork."

"Well, speaking of that…"

"What?" I asked, curious where that was leading.

Joey sighed and began, "At my dad's funeral, there were all these people and soldiers and stuff. They even fired rifles. And when it was almost over, my mom and me and the rest of our family were out there in the cemetery sitting in front of the coffin. And the priest comes over to us. And he's going down the front row shaking our hands and saying stuff. And people are crying. And he gets to me, and he shakes my hand and says, 'It's good to see you here, son.' And you know what I said?"

"No, what?"

"It's great to be here," Joey said, shaking his head.

I wanted to laugh, but that might have made it worse. So, I bowed my head and didn't say anything.

"And he just looked at me," Joey continued. "I felt like such a dork. I didn't mean it the way it sounded. I just didn't know what I was supposed to say."

"I've never been to a funeral before," I said, "so I wouldn't know what to say either."

"It just came out all wrong. I felt bad. I mean, what would my dad think?"

I gave that question serious thought for a moment. "I didn't know your dad," I said, "but maybe he'd think it was funny and tell you not to worry about it."

Joey gave me a look of surprised enlightenment. "I think I'll go with that," he said, with a smile.

"Hey, look who's coming down the street," I said, spotting Joni over Joey's shoulder.

"Hey!" she said with a wave.

"What are you up to?" I asked.

"I was coming to see if you wanted to go out on the beach and look for sharks' teeth. It's low tide."

"What do you think, Joey?" I asked.

"Sure, I'm game. I might go swimming while you guys hunt for teeth, though."

Joni and Joey turned to walk back in the direction of King's, and I followed. Joni asked Joey about the funeral, and he said it went fine without telling her the "great to be here" story. As we reached the cut-through to the beach that led past Mr. Wilson's, Joey turned up the path.

"Let's don't go that way," I said, stopping.

"Aw, come on," he said, without slowing down.

Joni went right along with Joey without question.

"All right," I said, following them up the path, "but if Mr. Wilson starts yelling again, I'm blaming you."

"Look, he's not even out there," said Joey, pointing to Mr. Wilson's deck.

"Good," I said. "That guy gives me the creeps."

We made it all the way up the path free of sandspurs, and my mind was already drifting toward sharks' teeth. I wanted to find the biggest gray tooth ever and give it to Joni.

Just as we reached the base of the dunes, Joni stopped and said, "Oh my gosh." She pointed toward the dunes directly in front of Mr. Wilson's house. "I think that's a dead cat over there."

About halfway up the dune, a black and white cat lay motionless on its side. Before I could say a word of caution, Joni was heading off the path to investigate. Joey and I followed.

"Can you imagine what Old Man Wilson will do if he catches us over here?" I asked Joey.

"I'm not worried," he said. "There's three of us. I don't think he'd hurt a girl, and I'm faster than you."

"Very funny."

Joni had knelt down on the sand and was leaning over the cat, poking it with a stick of seagrass. "It's dead, all right."

I looked at the poor cat's open yellow eyes. "I wonder what happened to it," I said.

"Old Man Wilson probably killed it just like he killed his wife," said Joey.

"Oh, stop it," said Joni. "It's probably his cat. We should let him know we found it."

"How would we do that?" asked Joey. "I'm not waiting around for Mr. Wilson to come out."

"We could leave a note," I suggested.

"Where?" asked Joey.

"On the cat," I said, beginning to lose confidence in my idea, already.

"What good would that do?" asked Joey. "He'd probably think we killed it."

"We won't sign our names," I offered.

Joni hopped up from the sand and brushed off her knees while Joey and I continued our pointless debate.

"But if he finds the cat," argued Joey, "he'll know it's dead without even reading the note."

Joni began to walk back toward the path.

"Where are you going?" I asked her.

"To knock on his door," she said, without looking back.

"Wait!" I said, "What if Mr. Wilson is home?"

"That's the whole reason I'm going to knock," she said glancing back at me. "So, I can tell him about the cat."

Joey and I hurried along behind her up the stairs to the deck overlooking the dunes. Without hesitation, Joni knocked on the front door. From inside, I heard the faint sound of a woman's voice calling for help.

"Did you hear that?" I asked.

"It sounded like someone calling for help," said Joey.

"Hello?" said Joni as she knocked again.

"Help!" said the faint voice inside.

"There it is again," said Joey. "It's a lady. She needs help."

"What should we do?" asked Joni.

"I could go get my aunt," I suggested.

Joey put his hand on the doorknob. "The door's unlocked, he said. "I'm going in."

"Are you crazy?" I said as Joey opened the door.

"Hello?" said Joey, stepping inside.

I followed closely behind Joey as he entered the house. I felt Joni's hand on my back. I wasn't sure if she was pushing me inside or just staying connected. Once inside, we fanned out shoulder to shoulder. In front of us sat a woman in a wheelchair smoking a cigarette. She was facing a television set, but it wasn't turned on. A silver oxygen tank sat on the floor next to her wheelchair with a clear tube running off behind it.

"Oh, thank goodness," the woman said. "Can one of y'all hand me my mask?"

"Your mask?" asked Joey.

"I dropped it on the floor, and I can't reach it. Right here beside my chair."

Joey stepped over to her chair and found a clear mask attached to the tube and handed it to her. With her cigarette in one hand and the mask in the other, she pressed the mask to her face and took a deep breath. When she removed it, she coughed the air out of her lungs and repeated the process one more time. She then relaxed in her chair and took a puff from her cigarette.

"Thank you, child," she said to Joey. "I don't know what I would've done if you hadn't come by. My husband's gone to the store."

"Why do you have to breathe in that mask?" Joni asked.

"I have emphysema," she said. "Probably from smoking." She chuckled to herself.

"Is that why you're in the wheelchair?" I asked.

"I'm in the wheelchair because I have MS."

"What's MS?" I asked.

"Multiple sclerosis," she said. "My legs don't work anymore. Oh, I think I hear Frank coming up the stairs now."

We turned toward the door and waited for it to open. When it did, we all took a step backward. Mr. Wilson stopped in the open doorway, a grocery bag in each arm, and glared at us. The surprise on his face faded to anger in less than a second.

"What are you kids doing in here?" he asked, placing the groceries on a table just inside the door.

None of us said anything.

He pointed his finger at Joey and me. "You're the two boys that were on my dunes." He took a strong step toward us.

"They were helping me, Frank," the lady said, stopping him in his tracks. "I had dropped my mask, and they heard me calling for help."

He studied us for a moment. "Who are you kids?" he asked, looking at Joni.

"I'm Joni Skinner."

"Carlton's daughter?" he asked.

"Yes, sir."

He looked at Joey next.

"I'm Joey Cotton, sir."

"Cotton. Was your daddy the soldier they just brought home?"

"Yes, sir."

"I'm sorry for your loss, son."

"Thank you, sir."

"How about you?" he asked looking at me.

"My name's Ran Fox."

"Fox?" he asked, with interest.

"Yes, sir."

"You any relation to Breland Fox?"

"He's my uncle. I'm just staying at his house for the summer."

Mr. Wilson backed up slowly, reaching behind him until he found his leather recliner, then took a seat. He looked at his wife, then back at me. "How'd y'all come to hear her calling for help? I can barely hear her from the next room."

"They knocked on our door, Frank," said his wife.

"You kids selling something?" he asked.

"No, sir," said Joni. "We found a dead cat in front of your house. We thought it might be yours."

"Was it black and white?" he asked.

"Yes, sir," said Joni.

"You sure it was dead?"

"Yes, sir," she said. "Its face was all grimaced and its teeth were showing."

"And his eyes were open," I added.

"Is it yours?" asked Joni.

"Not really," he said. "I just fed it. It's one of those cats that just does its own thing." He then turned his attention back to me. "So, I'm guessing your uncle doesn't know you're here."

"No, sir," I said. His question made me a little nervous. "We didn't plan on this."

"You said you're staying with him for the summer?"

"Yes, sir."

"Are you Tommy's boy?" he asked.

"Tom Fox is my dad, yes, sir. We live in Columbia."

He looked at me for a moment, while he processed whatever was going on in his head. "I'm surprised Breland..." He stopped mid-sentence, then asked, "How's your uncle been with you staying here?"

"He didn't like it at first," I said. "But it's getting better."

"Has he mentioned Bobby?"

"Just one time. But I don't know who Bobby is."

"Bobby was your uncle's son."

That came as a bit of a shock. I wasn't even sure if I believed him at first. "I didn't know he had a son," I said.

"Bobby died twelve years ago when he was about your age. You're eleven or twelve, aren't you?"

"Almost thirteen. Yes, sir," I said. The question I was about to ask next scared me, but it came out anyway. "How did Bobby die?"

Mr. Wilson stood up from his chair. "Thank y'all for helping my wife," he said, ignoring my question. "I know Emma appreciated that."

His wife nodded and smiled. "Y'all are welcome here any time," she said.

"Let me show you out," he said, herding us slowly toward the door.

Joey and Joni walked ahead of me, but before I could get out the door, Mr. Wilson placed his hand on my shoulder and turned me around. "Son, do me a favor, would you?" he asked.

"Sure," I said. "I mean, yes, sir." I watched him lower himself to one knee in front of me, keeping his hand on my shoulder.

He looked intensely into my eyes and said, "I want you to tell your uncle Breland…that Frank Wilson said…that he was sorry. Will you tell him that for me?"

"Yes, sir."

"Promise?"

"I promise."

"Thank you, son."

TWENTY-FIVE

Everything I Own

After leaving Mr. Wilson's house, we headed for the beach going up and over his dunes. He must not have seen us, or maybe he gave us a free pass for helping his wife. Regardless, I wasn't sure what to make of Mr. Wilson now that I'd met him. He reminded me of Uncle Breland. Stern, serious, a little scary, but surprisingly nice at times. Grown-ups could be so hard to figure out. The tide was out so the water was a long way from the dunes. Joni steered us along to where she thought we'd find the most shark's teeth.

"So, I guess Old Man Wilson's not so mean after all," said Joey as we walked toward the waterline. "At least we know he didn't kill his wife."

"Or the cat," added Joni.

"I'm a little freaked out that he knew my dad," I said.

"Why?" asked Joni. "He knew my dad. Nothing freaky about that."

"Yeah, but you're from here; I'm not."

"It's OK," said Joey, in a consoling tone. "We like you anyway."

"I think it's sweet that he takes care of his wife like that," said Joni.

"Let's see how sweet he is when we go back over his dunes later," said Joey.

"Let's not push our luck," I said. "That's enough Mr. Wilson for today."

"That's cool," said Joey, taking off his shirt. "Here, hold this."

Joey left me with his shirt and ran off into the surf. Joni had already turned her attention to the sand below her feet. Watching her look for sharks' teeth, while pretending to do the same, I realized how much Joni had grown on me. Without Joey around for those few weeks, I had spent more time with her than anyone. She made it easy to just hang around. And I felt comfortable acting my age around her, which I didn't with Heather. Although, when I first started sitting on the barstool and talking with Joni while she worked, I was a little worried about being a nuisance. I mean, she was trapped there. It was kind of her job to talk to me. But when she invited me to sit behind the counter it changed everything. It was like having a friend from home at the beach. While we laughed at the same things and liked the same kind of food, we didn't share the same taste in music. She liked country, which I didn't. She even tried to convince me that Olivia was a country singer. I argued that if she was, then why did I hear her songs on regular radio stations? "That just proves how good she is," Joni said. And suddenly we were on the same page again.

"I found one," she said, holding her palm out to me.

The tooth in her hand was perfectly shaped, but not much bigger than a grain of rice. "How did you even find that?" I asked. "It's tiny."

"You just have to know what you're looking for," she said, smiling.

I gave an instinctive grunt and turned my full attention to the sand. Despite walking all the way to the north end, with Joey drifting along with us in the water, I didn't find a single tooth. Joni found three more. I finally gave up. We spent the rest of the afternoon in and out of the water as we slowly made our way back. Neither Joey nor I had any money for games, so we left Joni at King's and headed home.

I said goodbye to Joey and walked up the steps of the house. I waved to Uncle Breland as I passed through the porch but decided to talk with Aunt Sarah about Mr. Wilson before saying anything to him. Maybe she would have some wisdom she could share with me. Or maybe she could fill in some of the holes in the story, like what happened to Bobby. I found her in the kitchen, frying chicken.

I told Aunt Sarah about the dead cat and the three of us going into Mr. Wilson's house. While she listened, she moved the chicken around the frying pan with a fork but stayed quiet. When I had told her everything, she simply said, "You need to tell your uncle what you just told me. But wait until after supper. OK, hon?" I love my aunt, but that turned out to be a complete waste of time.

At the supper table, I kept my mouth full of chicken, rice and gravy, and green beans to avoid talking. Aunt Sarah did her best to make conversation with Uncle Breland, who was even more stoic than usual. After I finished eating, I asked permission to be excused and retreated into my bedroom. I closed the door, grabbed *Where the Red Fern Grows* off the nightstand, and found my folded page corner. I would talk to Uncle Breland, but I felt the need to procrastinate a little bit first.

I was almost finished with the book. Billy was home from winning the championship and was off hunting again with his dogs. There weren't many pages left, so I settled into what I thought was the happy ending to the story. But then the mountain lion appeared. I began reading faster, while at the same time wanting to stop. I didn't want to know what came next but kept turning pages. I couldn't believe it. Old Dan died saving Billy from the lion. I felt a mix of grief and anger as I held the book in my hands. It wasn't supposed to end that way. But then it got worse. Little Ann stopped eating and died from a broken heart. She couldn't live without Old Dan. And Billy had to bury them both.

I closed the book for a moment and looked at the ceiling. A single tear ran past my ear and onto my pillow. I didn't understand why I was being forced to read that story. But with just a few pages left, I opened it again and finished reading. There was no happy ending. Only a sign of hope that a prayer had been answered. The end.

I tossed the book across the room onto the floor and sat up on the bed. Uncle Breland was on the porch by now, I figured, smoking his after-supper cigarette. Talking to him couldn't be any worse than the book, so I hopped off my bed and opened my door. Aunt Sarah was busy cleaning the kitchen as I slipped past her on my way to the porch.

"Hey, Uncle Breland," I said, finding him just as I thought I would.

He nodded and stared straight ahead, as usual, holding his cigarette between his fingers.

I sat down next to him and asked, "Can I talk with you for a minute?"

"What about?"

"Well," I said, pausing for a second before I dove in, "you know Mr. Wilson?"

My uncle looked at me. "Frank Wilson?"

"Yes, sir."

He took a puff of his cigarette. "Were you on his dunes, again? I heard the jerk yelled at you."

"No, sir. I was in his house."

It wasn't often that I got a noticeable reaction from Uncle Breland, but I sure did that time. He stiffened in his chair, looked at me, and said, "What the…" Unsatisfied with the blank look on my face, he twisted in his rocking chair toward the den. "Sarah! Did you know this boy was in Frank Wilson's house?"

"Yes," Aunt Sarah replied from the kitchen.

Clearly frustrated with her simple answer, Uncle Breland mashed the lit end of his cigarette on the arm of his chair, flicked it away, and stared at me with those intense eyes of his. "What were you doing in that son of a…what were you doing in his house?"

"Well, there was this dead cat."

"In his house?"

"No, on the dunes in front of his house. And Joni thought we should tell Mr. Wilson in case it was his cat. So, she knocked on his door. And that's when we heard Mrs. Wilson calling for help."

"Calling for help?"

"Yes, sir. Mr. Wilson wasn't home, so Joey opened the door. She was in a wheelchair in their den, and she had dropped her mask."

"What mask?"

"She has to hold this mask on her face to help her breathe in between puffs on her cigarettes. She had dropped it and couldn't reach it. And there was this big tank of oxygen next to her."

"It's a wonder she doesn't blow up their whole damn house."

"Why would she do that?"

"Never mind. What happened?"

"So, anyway, Mr. Wilson came home when we were there and got awfully mad at us. But Mrs. Wilson told him what happened and that we were just trying to help. He asked my name, and when I told him, he asked if I was your nephew. And he knew my dad too."

"Go on."

"Well, Aunt Sarah had told me to stay away from him, so I was kind of surprised he knew you."

My uncle turned his head away from me and threw his gaze back to the ocean. He took a long time before he said anything else. I didn't know if I should keep talking or just wait. Waiting seemed like the safer choice.

"Frank Wilson was the best man in my wedding," he said without looking at me.

"But Aunt Sarah said she'd never met him."

"She hasn't. Your aunt Sarah wasn't your first aunt. I was married once before. Before you were born."

"Oh. I guess that's how he knew my dad."

"What else did he tell you?"

"He told me you had a son named Bobby." I watched my uncle's face flush with emotion. It reminded me of when we sat together by the creek. "And he made me promise to tell you that he's sorry," I added.

His eyes stayed on mine, unblinking, as they filled with tears. "Frank said that?"

"Yes, sir. He said to tell you that Frank Wilson said he was sorry."

We sat there on the porch in our chairs without talking or rocking. The light was almost gone from the evening sky, and you could barely hear the waves rolling onto the beach over the cicadas all around us. When my uncle finally spoke again, the emotion had left his face.

"We all went fishing that morning in the creek, down at the south end," he said, staring toward the ocean. "Me, Bobby, and Frank. We were there for a couple of hours, I guess. I promised my wife I'd catch supper. But nothing was biting, and Bobby got a little bored. He was about your age and wanted to go swimming instead of holding a fishing pole. At first, he jumped in right where I was fishing, but I told him to move further down the creek. I don't like people swimming where I'm fishing. Besides, the current was taking my line right to him. So, he got out and walked around the bend to the left where the creek widens a bit. I told him to stay where I could see him. A few minutes later I heard some yelling. It sounded like somebody was in trouble. I dropped my pole and ran as fast as I could. People were pointing to the water. Bobby was in the middle of the creek. The tide was going out and the current had caught hold of him. I ran as fast as I could along the shore and managed to get ahead of him before I went in, thinking I could cut him off. The water was moving so fast. But I got to him, and I grabbed his arm."

"And you said, 'I got you, Bobby.'"

He nodded. "But I didn't know Frank had been running right behind me. After I grabbed Bobby, Frank grabbed me. When he did, I...the tug from Frank... Bobby's arm slipped out of my hand." Uncle Breland looked down at his hands. His tears fell on them.

I sat there without moving, watching him struggle to finish his story. I stayed quiet and waited.

"And he was gone," he finally said. "We never found him."

As I listened, I could have inserted my name for Bobby's. Uncle Breland had to live through the same experience with me.

And it didn't seem fair that I lived, and Bobby didn't. "Uncle Breland...I'm sorry I put you through that all over again. Bobby should be sitting here with you, not me."

He placed his hand on my forearm and gave it a firm squeeze. "I know I wasn't that welcoming to you. But I'm glad you're here, Ran. I really am. I hope..."

He didn't finish his thought. Instead, he turned his eyes back toward the ocean. I realized that was the first time Uncle Breland had ever called me by my name. We didn't say anything else. He was slow to remove his hand from my forearm as he began to rock gently back and forth in his chair.

I had a new understanding of how *Where the Red Fern Grows* ended. Sometimes, all you have to cling to is hope.

TWENTY-SIX

Free Ride

I must have slept pretty hard after my talk with Uncle Breland. It took a few blinks to get my eyes to stay open, but I was awake. And hungry. The light in my room told me the sun had been up for a while. From the other side of my door, I could hear the wonderful sizzle of something in a frying pan. I slid slowly off my bed, crossed the room, and opened my door. Aunt Sarah was at the stove, her back to me.

"There he is," my aunt said, glancing over her shoulder. "Are you hungry?"

"Yes, ma'am," I said, plopping down at the kitchen table.

"How about some French toast with fresh strawberries?"

"Sounds amazing," I said through a yawn.

"Did you sleep good?" she asked.

"I don't know, I was asleep," I said, half-joking.

"I'll take that as a yes," she said, chuckling. When she had finished cooking, she served up two big pieces of French toast on a plate with a bottle of Aunt Jemima, a bowl of sliced strawberries, and a glass of cold milk.

"Where's Uncle Breland?" I asked, not seeing him on the porch.

"He had to go take care of something this morning. He'll be back after a while."

"Can I have all these strawberries?" I asked.

"Yes, you may," she said with a smile. She seemed a little more chipper than usual for some reason. "After you finish eating, come into the den. I want to show you something."

"Yes, ma'am," I said, as I dumped the whole bowl of strawberries on top of my toast. After dousing the pile on my plate with syrup, I went to work. I had no plans for the day, nothing to read, no TV to look at, and no radio to listen to. It's no wonder I can remember every bite of my breakfast.

When I had finished, I cleaned up the best I could and joined Aunt Sarah in the den. She was sitting on the couch, reading a copy of TV Guide magazine. Yes, TV Guide. In the house with no TV. Johnny Carson's picture was on the cover. I guess she was trying to imagine what it was like to be entertained.

"Sit here next to me, hon," she said, patting the seat cushion.

While I took my place on the couch, she reached over to the end table and pulled a photograph out of the drawer. She placed it on the coffee table in front of us but didn't say anything. I leaned over to get a good look. It was the same picture I saw hanging on the wall in Ms. Mary's trailer.

"I saw this picture at Ms. Mary's," I said.

She pointed to the boy in the picture. "That's your cousin Bobby."

"That's Bobby?" I said, looking closer. "Who's the lady?"

"That's Ms. Mary. She was a lot younger then. She was Bobby's mother."

It took me a second to connect the dots, but I got it. "You mean, Uncle Breland was married to Ms. Mary?"

My aunt nodded.

"What happened?"

She thought for a second before answering. "You're a little young to understand this," she started, "but sometimes, losing a child can be too much for a couple. Every time they look at each other...the pain just never goes away. So, your uncle and Mary went their separate ways."

"But how did you get married to Uncle Breland?"

"Well, I met your uncle at the cemetery, of all places. We were both there for the same reason. Leaving flowers for someone we lost. Your uncle has never gotten over losing Bobby. He blames himself. He blames Frank Wilson. They haven't spoken for twelve years. But I want you to know that last night was the first time he's talked about Bobby since I don't know when."

"Wow," I said. "Did you know about Uncle Breland saving me in the creek?"

"Not until he told me last night, after you two talked."

"I knew he was upset after he pulled me out. I just didn't understand why."

"You do now, though."

"Yes, ma'am."

"Ran, underneath all that…" She stopped and thought for a second. "Let me say it a different way. Underneath the Uncle Breland you know is a warm, kind, thoughtful man. You're here for a few more weeks. Maybe, you'll get to see that side of him."

"I hope so," I said. Given the serious nature of our discussion, I'd been putting off saying something for as long as possible. But it couldn't wait any longer. "I have to go the bathroom."

Aunt Sarah excused me, and I ran to my bathroom to freshen up a bit, as my mom liked to say. When I returned to the den a few minutes later, Aunt Sarah told me Uncle Breland was back and needed me downstairs. The thought of seeing my French toast and strawberries again crossed my mind. Nevertheless, I headed out onto the porch and started down the stairs hoping there were no dead fish waiting for me. Uncle Breland was standing next to his pickup truck.

"Hey, Uncle Breland," I said, reaching the bottom of the stairs. "Aunt Sarah said you needed me."

"I just need your help getting something out of the back of my truck," he said, moving toward the tailgate.

"Sure," I said, meeting him at the back of his truck.

He pointed to the gate and said, "Just lift up on that handle there, and it'll come right down."

I lifted the handle and let the gate fall open in my hands. In the truck bed, lying on its side, was a red and white Schwinn Flying Star bicycle.

"I'll grab the back if you can grab the handlebars," he said.

Together, we lifted the bike out of the truck and stood it before us.

"What do you think?" Uncle Breland asked.

"Is this the same bike that was under the stairs?"

"Yep. I cleaned it up this morning. Greased the chain and put on some new tires. It should ride just fine. Why don't you try it out?"

"Really?"

"Sure, take her for a ride."

I had a bike at home, but it was totally different. Mine was a wheelie bike with a small front tire, big back tire, high-rise handlebars, and a banana seat. It was fun for popping wheelies and looking cool, but the Flying Star was a cruiser. It rode smooth and heavy as I peddled past King's and down to the north end of the road. In no time, I was back at the house. Uncle Breland was still standing beside his truck. It looked like he had a real smile on his face.

"How'd it ride?" he asked.

"Great!" I said, hopping off the bike.

"This was Bobby's bike," he said, holding the handlebar. "But it's yours whenever you're here at the beach."

"Wow, thank you, Uncle Breland!"

"You're very welcome."

"Ran," called Aunt Sarah from the porch, "In a little while, I have to go up to Surfside to pick up a few things. How would you like to come with me?"

"Um, no thanks," I said.

"I could drop you off at the new water park while I run my errands," she added.

She should have led with that. "That sounds great!" I said, changing my tone. "Can my friend Joey come?"

"That's fine with me," she said.

"Uncle Breland, can I ride the bike over to Joey's house to see if he can go with us?"

"Take off!" he said. "But be careful."

"Yes, sir!" I said, hopping on the bike.

I peddled away with a smile on my face as my aunt yelled from the porch, loud enough for half the island to hear, "Brush your teeth when you get back!"

TWENTY-SEVEN

Smoke on the Water

One of my first summer memories is playing in a baby pool in our backyard. I don't know how old I was, but I remember riding down a small plastic slide, splashing head-first into a foot of cold water. It was thrilling. I was the king of my own water park. Then our neighbor's Golden Retriever decided to join the fun. I tried to get him out, but he was just as determined to stay in as I was. And he was bigger than me. In the course of our resulting wrestling match, we flattened one side of the pool, spilling all the water into the grass. He ran back to his own yard, happy to have ruined my fun. I assume a responsible adult was watching all this, but they aren't part of the memory.

Riding a bike to Joey's house was a lot more fun than driving the truck. The flat road along the creek and the south causeway bridge were easy pedaling, with no worries about running over squirrels or being spotted by police. And I was pretty sure I could find his house again, even though everything looked different in the daylight. I remembered Joey's directions. Second right after the creek, then the first right after that. I recognized his house, but I had thought it was white, not yellow. Everything else looked right, though. I coasted to a stop, leaned the bike against his mailbox, and walked across the yard to the front door. Joey's mom answered the doorbell but told me he wasn't home. He was crabbing, she said. Then without asking who I was or any further conversation, she closed the door. I turned around and stepped off the porch. I wondered if Joey was back at the same boardwalk on the creek trying to steal that man's crabs. The thought got my feet moving quickly toward the bike.

The mental image of Joey sitting in the back of a police car pushed my pedals a lot faster on the way back. When I finally came to a skidding stop at the boat ramp next to the boardwalk, Joey wasn't there. I'd missed him, or he was already on his way to jail. Either way, I didn't like the idea of going to the water park alone. So, I rode back to the house ready to decline my aunt's invitation. But when I got there, I was happy and surprised to see Joey sitting at the bottom of our stairs.

"Hey!" I said, hopping off my bike. "I was just looking for you."

"Hey," said Joey, sounding a little down. "Nice bike."

"Yeah!" I said, with a little more enthusiasm than I intended. "It's old, but my uncle fixed it up for me. What's up with you? You OK?"

"I got caught," he said, looking up at me.

"Stealing crabs from that man?"

"Yeah."

I sat down on the stairs next to him. "Did you get arrested?"

"No. He came out and started yelling at me. He didn't know who I was, so...I kind of lied."

"What did you say?"

"I told him I was you."

"You did what?!"

"Well, I couldn't have him take me home to my mom. She's been through enough lately. So, I told him I was staying here for the summer. I was hoping he'd just let me go, but he brought me over here. He wanted to speak to my dad, he said."

"Was my uncle Breland here?"

"Yeah, he came down. I was kind of worried about what he'd say. But he was cool. He covered for me. He just said that he'd take care of it. And the jerk went home."

"Is Uncle Breland upstairs?"

"No, he left. He said you'd be right back, so I thought I'd wait."

I noticed Uncle Breland's truck was still at the house. "Do you know where he went?" I asked.

"He said something about taking his own advice and walked down that way." Joey pointed down the street. "I saw him go up the path toward Mr. Wilson's house."

Uh-oh, I thought. "What advice was he talking about?" I asked.

"Well, we sat on the steps here, and he told me he was sorry about my dad. And he asked why I was stealing the crabs. When I explained it to him, he said I shouldn't waste my youth holding grudges. It's a waste of time, he said. He told me you've got to just keep living. He said that's what my dad would want me to do. Then he stood up and said he was going to take his own advice. And he left."

"And you think he went to Mr. Wilson's?"

"He went that way, yeah. Why?"

"My aunt said he blames Mr. Wilson for his son drowning in the creek."

"His son drowned in the creek? When did that happen?"

"About twelve years ago. I think."

"Oh, man," said Joey, shaking his head.

"Yeah," I said. After a brief moment of silence, I asked, "Hey, you want to go to the water park?"

"When?"

"Like, now. I think."

"Sure!"

We went up the stairs and into the house to find Aunt Sarah. She wasn't on the porch or in the kitchen, and her bedroom door was closed.

Joey looked around the den as we stood waiting for her to appear. "That's the TV that doesn't work?" he asked.

"Yeah," I said.

"So, you missed Andy Kim singing, *Rock Me Gently* last Saturday on *Bandstand*?"

"Who's Andy Kim?"

"You don't have a radio around here either?"

"No."

"You're really out of it, aren't you?"

Aunt Sarah came out of her bedroom carrying two towels and wearing shoes on her feet. I knew that meant she was ready to go.

"Aunt Sarah, this is my friend Joey," I said.

"Sure, we met at the supermarket," she said. "I'm so sorry about your dad."

"Thank you, ma'am."

"Are you boys ready to go?"

"Just one sec," I said. I ran to my bedroom, grabbed a five-dollar bill from the floor, and stuffed it in my pocket.

We followed Aunt Sarah down the stairs to her car.

"Here are a couple of towels to sit on after the water park," she said.

We each took a towel and climbed into the car. I claimed the front seat, so I could play the radio. Joey sat in the back. The vinyl seats were hot, so we both sat on our towels. Once Aunt Sarah started the car, I turned on the radio.

"What stations are good around here?" I asked Joey.

"Try WTGR, Tiger Radio. It's 1450 AM. It's the best one."

"Tiger Radio?" I asked, as I turned the dial.

"Yeah, they play all the Top 40 stuff."

Just as I hit 1450, Joey got excited.

"This is the song!" he said.

"What song?"

"*Rock Me Gently* by Andy Kim!"

My aunt Sarah was a good sport. She let me turn up the volume and smiled as Joey sang along with Andy Kim. It didn't take me long to learn the chorus and loudly join in.

Rock me gently!
Rock me slowly!
Take it easy, don't you know!
That I have never been loved like this before!

We were just a couple of minutes into our ride, and I had a new favorite song. The rest of the twenty-minute drive up to the water park wasn't quite as eventful. My aunt asked typical grown-up questions about the upcoming school year, which always shattered the summer illusion every kid held that school really didn't exist. But Joey and I played along, thankful for the ride. When we finally got there, we jumped out of the car, promised to be careful, and took in our surroundings.

The water park was really just a water slide. But it was the coolest thing I'd ever seen. It had three painted concrete chutes curving back and forth from the top of a big grassy hill to a small swimming pool at the bottom. We paid two dollars each to slide for an hour. I paid for Joey since he didn't have any cash. Plus, he had spent about that much losing to me in air hockey. So, we called it even.

When you paid, they assigned you a certain color mat to ride on. Ours were light green. When your hour was up, the lifeguard at the pool would collect your mat as you got out. There was a big clock on the outside of the little shack where you paid. I wasn't sure when my aunt would be back to pick us up, but if she was longer than an hour we'd be waiting where the grown-ups sat watching younger people have fun.

After grabbing our mats, Joey and I walked up the sidewalk to the top of the hill and got in line. We watched people slide down the three chutes while we waited. The chute on the right was clearly the slowest ride of the three, so the lines were longer for the center and left side. We didn't mind waiting. Speed was everything.

We tried a few different ways to slide down the hill. It was a steady progression in thrill-seeking. The first time down, we sat on our mats with our legs straight out in front of us. After getting that technique out of the way, we nicknamed it "Elmo" because it was for three-year-olds. To make up for Elmo, for our second slide down we held our mats by the top corners and dove into the chute headfirst. Of course, Joey named that the Superman. I suggested Aquaman instead since we were in water, but he was a little more passionate about it than I was.

Since the center and left chutes ran parallel, we raced each other doing the Superman (i.e., the Aquaman) for the next five or six rides down. It seemed like we tied every time, which led to half-hearted arguments over who won. And the lifeguard refused to get involved.

Since racing failed to produce bragging rights, we just went freestyle. Joey liked to ride upright, like a surfer on his knees. My favorite was what I called the Bizarro because it was like an upside-down Superman. I'd lay flat on my back with my head pointed downhill. There was no anticipation of the curves or the pool at the end because you couldn't see them coming, which made the whole ride more exciting. Just don't try to dive backward onto your mat to get started. Trust me. Really bad idea.

Back at the top of the hill, we stood waiting impatiently for a group of new, dry riders, who lacked our forty-five minutes of sliding experience, to figure out how to launch themselves into the chute.

"Look at these clowns," said Joey.

We both laughed and shook our heads. We had become water park snobs. That's when I heard, "Well, if it isn't Heather's old boyfriend."

We both turned around to find Ronny and a friend in line behind us. Since they didn't allow Golden Retrievers in the water park, Ronny stepped in to ruin my day.

"Take a hike, Ronny," said Joey.

"We're not going anywhere, dork," said Ronny's friend.

"Just ignore him," I said, trying to be the adult.

"Play any air hockey, lately?" asked Joey, looking up at Ronny.

"Hey, I just let the kid win because I felt sorry for him."

OK, it was on. "Yeah, tell that to Heather," I said. "While you're at it, ask her how she likes orange snow cones."

"What's that supposed to mean?" asked Ronny, bowing up as he took a step toward me.

"Hey, guys!" said an older boy who worked there. "Take a chill pill, will ya? Keep it fun or you're gonna have to leave."

The four of us turned away from each other without speaking. I was up next at the center chute. I decided to take my sweet time getting my Bizarro ready just to make Ronny wait. I turned around and placed my mat at the top of the chute, holding it with my foot. Just as I began to lie down backwards, Ronny kicked my mat out from underneath me. I fell into the chute with the water rushing over me, as Ronny and his little minion laughed at me. As I struggled to roll over and get moving somehow, Ronny leaped into the chute Elmo-style. He pushed me with his feet, laughing all the way down as I rolled and spun in front of him until we both plopped into the pool.

When I surfaced from the water, Joey was standing by the lifeguard stand holding my mat. Ronny waded out ahead of me, giving his buddy a high five as he climbed the steps onto the sidewalk.

"Did you see that?" I asked Joey, taking my mat.

"Yeah," he said. "But I've got an idea."

"I'm not sure I like the sound of that," I said as we started walking slowly back up the hill.

"Look, they've got blue mats," said Joey, pointing ahead at our enemy.

"So?" I asked.

"That means they'll be here another hour. Their gonna start pulling our green mats in about ten minutes. So, here's what we do. I'll get in line behind Ronny, and you get behind Eric. As soon as they go, we'll get a running jump and Superman right behind them. We'll catch up to their Elmo butts and drop into the pool at the same time. But just before you hit the water, grab Eric's mat. I'll grab Ronny's. Then, when we're all underwater, hang onto Eric's mat and let your green mat float away. They'll grab our mats, and we'll have theirs. Then just get out of the pool like everything's normal. Got it?"

"So, when the time's up for the green mats," I surmised, "they'll have to leave."

"Exactly," said Joey. "And we get to stay for another hour."

"What happens if we get caught?" I asked. "You're already 0 for 1 today."

"We'll just say it was an accident, apologize, and give them their mats back. No big deal. Are you in?"

"I can never decide if you're the good guy or the bad guy."

"I'm the good guy," he said, proudly. "Always."

"Uh-huh," I said, still unsure.

It took another slide down and a quick walk back up the hill for us to get in line right behind Ronny and Eric. But once in position, Joey gave me the green light nod and we executed his plan to perfection. We both got out of the pool with their blue mats, casually and without looking around. Ronny and Eric pushed past us on their way up the hill for another ride, carrying our mats.

"They didn't even notice," I said.

"See? I told, ya!" said Joey. "Who's the mastermind?"

"You are," I said, laughing.

Once at the top of the hill, we waited in line for the two fast lanes. Ronny and Eric were a few people ahead of us.

"Look down there," Joey said, pointing to the pool. "They're starting to pull the green mats. Let's just wait up here and see what happens."

Joey and I moved out of line and let other kids go by.

"Hey, Ronny," Joey said, "you guys should try riding down on your stomachs. You go a lot faster."

"Thanks, squirt," said Ronny.

"No problem," said Joey, grinning.

Ronny and Eric both slid down Superman-style and splashed headfirst into the pool below. As they made their way out of the water, we watched as the lifeguard asked both of them for their mats. Ronny and Eric looked confused as the lifeguard pointed at the clock and then at their mats. All three walked over to the payment window and, after a brief discussion, they were given new blue mats.

"They're staying," I said to Joey, my anxiety rising. "What now?"

"I don't know," he said. "I didn't think about that."

"Mastermind, huh?"

Ronny and Eric turned their attention to the top of the hill and spotted us watching, holding blue mats. Eric pointed and took a quick step toward the hill. Ronny grabbed his arm and turned him around. It looked like they were debating something. Eric was pleading his case and pointing at us while Ronny countered. After a moment, they seemed to reach an agreement and began the walk up the hill.

"Should we slide down real fast and leave?" I asked the mastermind.

"No, let's wait here," said Joey, watching them intently.

"But they obviously know we took their mats."

"So? I'm not going to run from these guys. Just let me do the talking."

We held eye contact with Ronny and Eric as they approached. From the looks on their faces, this was going to go badly, I thought. I imagined a brawl with mats flying everywhere and innocent bystanders rolling down the hill. I felt my right hand clench into a fist. I knew Ronny would kick my butt, but I may have a chance with Eric. I just wasn't going to dance around like Muhammad Ali this time.

When they were still about ten feet away, Ronny said, "You guys stole our mats."

"Yep," said Joey, holding his ground as the boys stopped before us.

"Whose bright idea was that?" Ronny asked.

My eyes darted involuntarily toward Joey.

"Mine," said Joey.

"Well played," said Ronny, with a smile. He put out his hand and gave Joey five. "Now we both have another hour to slide."

"You guys wanna race?" asked Joey. "Losers buy snow cones?"

"You're on," said Ronny.

I stood there with my mouth hanging open, as the other three boys walked past me and got in line. What just happened? I turned around and joined them, still a bit confused. Joey and Ronny were already discussing Elmo vs. Superman vs. his knee surfer technique.

"I'm Eric, by the way," said Ronny's friend.

"I'm Ran."

"You're just down for the summer?"

"Yeah. From Columbia."

"Cool."

For the next hour, the four of us raced, slid, made fun of people, and ate snow cones. Grape, not orange. It was the best time I'd had all summer.

TWENTY-EIGHT

I'm Doing Fine Now

I rolled over, pulled my pillow from between my headboard rails, and opened my eyes. The sky outside my window was beginning to change color. I could close my eyes, go back to sleep, and dream of waking up to Aunt Sarah's pancakes. Or I could get out of bed and see if Joni was on the beach watching the sunrise. As a compromise, I decided to daydream about pancakes while I walked down to the beach to find Joni.

Some mornings before the sun came up, I'd find the beach totally empty. On other days, people and dogs would be scattered all up and down the shoreline. But I liked sitting with Joni when it was just the two of us. It felt like our beach. Our sunrise. And no one else's. That morning, I got my wish. It was just us. I saw her sitting in her usual spot at the bottom of the dunes, her arms wrapped around her knees, patiently waiting. She saw me coming.

"Hey," she said, as I walked toward her.

"Hey. Can I sit with you?"

"Of course," she said. "Just don't block my view."

I sat down beside her to her right to make sure I was out of the way.

"So, what's up?" she asked. "I haven't seen you in a couple days."

"Oh. Joey and I went to the water park yesterday."

"I haven't been, yet. How was it?"

"It was off the hook fun. We hung out with Ronny and this boy named Eric."

She turned her head toward me. Which, I'd learned, is unusual for her when the sun is about to come up. "You hung out with Ronny and Eric?"

"Yeah. Why?"

"Oh, nothing," she said, turning her head back to the horizon. "I just didn't see that coming."

"They're good guys. We had fun."

She seemed to be processing something as she stared straight ahead. "You seem like you've changed since you've been here," she finally said.

"Really? What do you mean?"

"I don't know. You were kind of hard to talk to at first."

"I was?"

She nodded and thought for a moment. "You seemed a little...distracted or...intense."

It was embarrassing to hear how I had come across. But I couldn't argue with what she was saying. "I was just being stupid, I guess."

"My grandpa says that getting up early to watch the sun come up makes you smarter."

"I hope it's working," I said.

"It must be," she said, smiling.

We sat there quietly for a few minutes, waiting. Even at the age of twelve-going-on-thirteen, there were some events or times that, even as they were happening, I hoped I would never forget. That morning with Joni was one of them. Sitting alone on the beach with her was so much better than dreaming about pancakes. Even Aunt Sarah's pancakes.

The sun put on a show for us that morning. The ocean was like a big sheet of glass, reflecting all the orange, yellow, blue, and white in the sun-painted sky.

"That was amazing," she said.

"I feel smarter, already," I said, smiling.

She stood up and brushed herself off. "What are you up to today?"

"I don't know," I said, rising to my feet.

"I'm working this afternoon if you want to come by," she said as we walked toward her pathway off the beach. "I'll save your barstool for you."

"You should just put my name on it," I said.

"I can do that, you know," she said, with a smile. "I'll see you later."

When I got back to the house, Uncle Breland was on the porch. Or at least I thought it was Uncle Breland. As I opened the screen door at the top of the stairs, I stopped and tried to reconcile what I was seeing. It looked like an aged version of my dad.

"You shaved off your mustache," I said.

"Time for a change," he said, holding a notepad on his lap and a pen in his hand.

"It looks good," I said, still amazed at the difference.

He nodded and didn't respond. At least that hadn't changed. He focused on his writing as I sat down a few chairs away.

"What are you writing?" I asked, being nosey.

"A letter to your father."

My heart did a quick drum solo inside my chest. "Did I do something wrong?"

"Nope," he said, simply.

"Oh," I said, still curious. "You're just saying hey?"

He turned his head to me and said, "After your father reads this, you can ask him what it says."

For Uncle Breland, that was about as nice a way to tell me to mind my own business and leave him alone as I could've imagined. I started to head to my room, when he said, "I'm going fishing later, if you want to come."

"Fishing?" I said, stopping behind my chair.

He nodded.

I had to think about that for a second. I'd never been fishing before. But the fact that he invited me to go with him was kind of a big deal. So, I said, "That sounds good."

"I'll let you know when I'm ready to go," he said, beginning to write again.

I went to my room and closed the door. Once on my bed, I nodded off for a little while, until I heard Aunt Sarah in the kitchen. The sounds of her banging pots and frying things filled my ears. I hopped off the bed to investigate.

"Morning, Aunt Sarah," I said, opening my door. "What's for breakfast?"

"Morning, Ran. I'm fixing grits and salmon and eggs," she said, lifting the lid off a pot on the stove.

I know what you're thinking: The combination of fish and eggs sounded questionable, but because it's Aunt Sarah, I just rolled with it. And you would be right. Still, Aunt Sarah must have noticed some hesitancy on my part.

"You can either have that or your cereal," she said. "Which do you prefer?"

That was easy. I was going fishing. And there's a history when it comes to Captain Crunch and fish. "I'll have the salmon and egg thing," I said.

"Ask Joey if he'd like some too," she said, stirring the grits. "He's on the porch with your uncle Breland."

"He is?"

"Hm-mm," she said. "Go see."

I walked through the den and found Joey sitting in a rocking chair next to my uncle.

"What did your father do before he left for Vietnam?" I heard my uncle ask.

"He worked at the steel mill in Georgetown," said Joey. "I'm not sure what he did there."

"Hey, Joey," I said, joining them. "When did you get here?"

"About ten minutes ago," he said. "I was up early and thought I'd stop by."

"You weren't stealing crabs again, were you?"

"No," he said, glancing at my uncle.

"Tell him," said Uncle Breland.

"Tell me what?"

"I went over to Captain Miller's house," said Joey.

"Is that the man with the crab trap?"

Joey nodded. "I went back over and told him who I was and that I was sorry for trying to steal his crabs. And I told him why too."

"What did he say?"

"He thanked me for coming back over. He invited me into his house and told me how much he thought of my dad."

"Did you ask him what happened to your dad?" I asked.

"I did. I told him I needed to know. My mom and I both need to know. He told me that my dad volunteered for a secret rescue mission. He said they got a tip on where some POWs were being held, and my dad offered to lead a few men to find them. But they didn't come back. He said at the time, they weren't supposed to be fighting anymore. There was a peace agreement or something. So, he said what they did was kind of against orders. That's why he couldn't talk about it until now."

"Why is now any different?" I asked.

"I guess because he's not in the military, anymore."

"Your father was a brave man," said Uncle Breland.

Joey nodded. "At least I know what happened, kind of."

"What made you want to go back over there?" I asked.

"I thought about what your uncle told me yesterday. You know, about not holding grudges. And what my dad would want me to do." Joey turned to Uncle Breland. "Thank you for the advice, Mr. Fox."

"I'm glad that helped you, son," said my uncle. "And how 'bout you just call me Uncle Breland? Makes things easy."

"OK," said Joey, smiling.

"Hey, Uncle Breland, can Joey go fishing with us?"

"That's fine with me."

"How 'bout it Joey?"

"I'm in!"

"Cool!"

Aunt Sarah joined us on the porch. "Is everybody ready to eat?" she asked.

Since the little table in the kitchen only had three chairs, we all ate breakfast together on the porch. I followed Uncle Breland's example and mixed my scrambled eggs and salmon together with my grits. It was a plate full of yellow and white mush, but it tasted great. Joey said his mom makes it the same way. I needed to have a serious conversation with my mom when I got home.

After we ate – and after I brushed my teeth – Joey and I followed Uncle Breland down to his truck. We helped him grab some fishing gear from the downstairs porch and loaded it into the truck bed.

"Joey, have you done much fishing?" Uncle Breland asked, lifting a cooler into the truck.

"My dad and I used to fish off the south causeway bridge a lot," said Joey.

"Do you remember what you fished for?" asked Uncle Breland.

"I think it was redfish. We used minnows for bait."

"That sounds right," Uncle Breland said. "Ran, how about you?"

"I've never been fishing before."

"Never?" asked Joey.

"Nope. My dad's too busy to do that kind of stuff."

"Well, I'll tell you what," my uncle said, looking at me. "Joey can teach you what he knows about fishing, and you can teach him how to drive my truck. Think you can do that?"

"Sure!" I said.

"All right, let's get in," said Uncle Breland.

I hopped in the truck on the driver's side and Joey sat in the middle. Uncle Breland leaned over and stuck the key in the ignition.

"OK," I said to Joey, "watch everything I do." I walked him through how to mash on the clutch pedal and shift gears, just like Uncle Breland showed me. I told him not to steer around squirrels and to always push in the clutch pedal at stop signs. Then I put it in reverse, backed us onto the street, and got us rolling forward. After we got on the creek road, I pulled over.

"You want to try?" I asked.

"Sure," Joey said. "Where are we going fishing?"

"Just drive us down to the south end," said Uncle Breland.

"Yes, sir."

Joey and I hopped out of the truck, then I jumped in next to Uncle Breland while Joey got in behind the wheel. His toes barely reached the pedals.

"You may want to scoot up a little closer to the steering wheel," I suggested.

After getting settled, Joey mashed the clutch to the floor and, after a couple of tries, found first gear. He was a little slow giving it gas as he lifted his foot off the clutch which caused the truck to jump forward and cut off.

I gave a quick look to Uncle Breland, but he stayed quiet. "That's OK," I told Joey. "Just give it more gas next time."

I told him how to start the engine and, in no time, he had us rolling down the street.

"Give it a little more gas," I told him. "And move the gear changer to second gear. It's straight up. Don't forget to mash the clutch pedal."

He shifted into second gear with ease and got us up to fifteen miles per hour. The smile on his face, as he steered us carefully around the first curve, told me he was enjoying himself. It was the first time I'd ever taught anyone to do anything. And I was having as much fun as Joey.

Once at the south end, we grabbed the cooler and all our fishing gear and followed Uncle Breland down to the creek. He picked a spot around the bend overlooking the marsh where the creek ran parallel to the street. While Uncle Breland got his own rod ready, Joey gave me a quick course on fishing.

"Sometimes at low tide, you'll see redfish tails splashing around over by the marsh grass. You want to cast your line so the current will take it right to them. If you cast where they're feeding, it will scare them off."

"This boy knows his redfish," said Uncle Breland. It was nice to actually see his smile without his mustache hiding it. "The bait is in a bucket in the cooler," he said, pointing. "We're fishing with shrimp today."

Joey opened the cooler, grabbed a shrimp for each of us, and baited our hooks. "Watch me, I'll show you," he said. With a smooth flick of his rod, his line went flying across the water into the marsh grass on the other side of the creek. "OK, that's not how you do it."

I actually heard Uncle Breland laugh out loud for the first time. It was a hearty laugh, ending with a short, smoker's cough. And it was contagious. I laughed with him while Joey reeled in his line.

"Hang on a sec," said Joey, resetting himself. He pointed across the creek near where his line went the first time. Something was splashing near the grass. "Did you see that?" He asked. "That was a redfish tail. He's feeding. Now watch."

This time, Joey cast his line about ten feet away from where the fish was feeding. I watched his line move slowly along with the current right to the fish. His pole suddenly bent like an upside-down U and almost pulled Joey into the water. Uncle Breland rushed over and held Joey steady while he fought with the fish.

With me cheering him on and Uncle Breland's help, Joey reeled in a redfish almost two feet long.

"Ran, take the cooler down to the water and fill it about halfway," my uncle said.

I reached into the cooler and took out the bucket of shrimp. After dunking the cooler in the creek, I dragged it back to Uncle Breland and Joey. They worked together to get the fish off the hook and into the cooler.

"I think we've got a fisherman, here," said my uncle, patting Joey on the back.

"That was great, Joey!" I said.

"That's the biggest fish I've ever caught," he said. "I wasn't expecting that."

"That's about as big as they get in these waters," said Uncle Breland.

"You boys caught something already?" I heard a man say behind us. I turned around and saw Mr. Wilson walking toward us.

"Hey Frank," said Uncle Breland. "I think we've got a future pro with us today."

Carrying a fishing pole and a small cooler, Mr. Wilson walked over to us and set his gear down beside Uncle Breland. The two of them smiled at each other and shook hands.

"We just got here a few minutes ago," my uncle said, "and Joey already landed a big one."

Mr. Wilson looked at the fish in the cooler, shook his head, and said, "I usually just call it a day when I catch something that big. Nice catch, son."

"Thank you, sir," said Joey.

"Breland, I appreciate Sarah looking after Emma this morning," said Mr. Wilson, picking up his fishing rod.

"She was happy to do it," said my uncle, baiting his hook.

"You look like the old Breland without the mustache," said Mr. Wilson.

"Thanks," said my uncle, rubbing his face. "I'm starting to feel like the old Breland too."

After Joey's big catch, I was excited to try my first cast. It didn't go very well. I let go of the line too late, and it splashed about ten feet in front of us.

"Try again," said Joey, chuckling. "You'll get the hang of it."

My next cast was much better, landing in the water near the marsh grass. I braced myself for the big tug on my line, but it never came. In fact, none of us caught another fish for the next hour. After Joey's catch, I thought we'd all be fighting massive fish all day, overflowing the cooler with enough food for a week. But instead, we all just sat on the sand, waiting. And waiting. I was getting bored.

"You want to go swimming?" asked Joey.

That sounded a zillion times more fun than fishing at that moment, but I needed to ask Uncle Breland. And I had a feeling he'd say no, all things considered.

"I'd like to, but..." I said, trying to be discreet. I motioned with my head toward Uncle Breland.

"But what?" asked Joey.

"I'm not sure that's a good idea," I said, whispering. "You know...Bobby."

"Just ask him."

I sighed, turned to my uncle, and said, "Hey, Uncle Breland, do you mind if Joey and I go swimming?"

Uncle Breland and Mr. Wilson both looked at me, with the same blank expression. Then they turned to each other and talked about something, but I couldn't hear what they were saying. Rather than answering me, Uncle Breland and Mr. Wilson both stood up and reeled in their lines. Then Uncle Breland dropped his pole and took off his shirt. "Why don't we all go swimming?" he said.

With that, both men ran and dove into the water.

Joey and I couldn't reel in our lines fast enough. But once we did, we sprinted into the water to join them. Joey climbed onto my uncle's shoulders, and I climbed onto Mr. Wilson's. We had wrestling matches to see who could throw the other off. Joey and Uncle Breland won 3-2. After that, we climbed up their backs and dove off their shoulders until we got tired. We didn't fish anymore that day, but we swam for a long time. It was more fun than the water park.

TWENTY-NINE

What's Going On

My last two weeks or so at the beach were the best of the whole summer. Whenever Joey wasn't working or helping his mom, he was hanging out with me. Some of that time we spent fishing with Uncle Breland and Mr. Wilson. I found that once I finally caught a fish, the initial boredom of fishing went away. From then on, time spent waiting for a bite felt more like hopeful anticipation. And it was fun.

My mom was coming to pick me up after the first full week in August on a Sunday. It was a week earlier than she had planned. She had let Aunt Sarah know, and she passed it on to me. She said something about needing more time to get ready for school, which I didn't really understand. I thought all you did was show up.

As my last weekend approached, I wanted to spend most of that Saturday at King's. But I had already used up the last of my $20 summer allowance. And since Joey was working that day, playing free air hockey wasn't an option. So, my plan was to just hang out with Joni. When I walked into the arcade, it seemed a lot busier than I had seen it all summer. Maybe everyone was trying to squeeze in whatever fun they could before school started. I walked over to the order window but didn't see Joni. So, I pulled up my barstool and waited to see if she was working.

"Hey, Ran!" I heard Joni say from behind me.

I turned around to see her coming in the arcade. "Hey! You're not working?"

"I am," she said. "You just beat me here. Hang on a sec."

She went through the door that said *Employees Only* and, after a moment, she appeared in the order window.

"So, when are you leaving?" she asked.

"Tomorrow," I said.

"Tomorrow?"

"Yeah. Around lunchtime, I think."

"Wow. Have you had a good summer?"

"You bet," I said. "It's been fun hanging out. And our sunrises were the bomb."

"Yeah," she said, fondly.

"We didn't get around to playing putt-putt though," I said.

She put on an air of confidence and said, "I would have just embarrassed you, anyway."

"Oh, you think so?" I said, laughing.

"Home court advantage," she claimed.

"I thought that was for basketball."

"It works for putt-putt too."

"Maybe we could play in the morning before I leave," I said. "We could watch the sun come up and–"

"I can't. Church."

"Oh," I said. "Well, shoot."

It began to really sink in that my time with Joni was almost over. While she took a little girl's order, I tried to think of anything that could keep my connection with her from ending.

After the girl got her popcorn, a boy about my age stepped up to the window. "Hey, Joni," he said.

"Hey, Alex," said Joni.

"Hey, um," Alex said slowly, "there's a big end-of-the-summer cook-out tomorrow afternoon at my church, and I was wondering if you'd like to go with me."

"Sure," said Joni, without hesitation. "That sounds fun."

"My dad's taking me," he said, "so we can swing by and pick you up around one o'clock. Is that OK?"

"That works for me!" said Joni, sounding excited.

"Groovy. See you tomorrow."

"Bye!" said Joni with a wave of her hand.

All of that happened right in front of me. I mean, a foot in front of me. Joni must have read the stupefied look on my face.

"What?" she asked. "What's wrong?"

"You're going with him?" I asked.

"Sure, why not," she said, casually wiping off the counter.

I held out my arms to prove I wasn't invisible. "I'm sitting right here," I said.

Joni stopped wiping and looked at me. "So? What am I missing?"

I sat struggling to form a coherent sentence.

"Oh, I get it," she said. "You don't think I should've said yes to Alex because you're here."

Why couldn't I have said that myself? "Yes," I said, trying to sound definitive.

"Ran, you're leaving tomorrow."

"I know, but I thought…" I honestly didn't know where I was going with that.

"You thought what?" she asked. "That I was your girlfriend?"

Wow, it was out there. I was glad she said it and not me. But now that it was up for discussion, I felt like I could make a strong case for it. "Well, we've spent a lot of time together, and I kind of assumed…"

"Ran, I like you. But I live here. I go to school with Alex. You're leaving tomorrow, and I might not ever see you again. It's been fun hanging out, like you said, but that's it."

As far as closing arguments go, I had no comeback for that one. But I still wasn't ready to give up. My time with Joni wasn't going to end like Aunt Sarah's story about Rory. "That's it?" I asked.

"Pretty much," she said.

I sat in quiet reflection for a moment. That's a fancy way of saying I was stalling for time. I quickly crossed off the idea of talking my parents into moving to the beach. So, as a last resort, I borrowed an idea from my uncle Breland and asked, "Can I write to you?"

She looked puzzled. "What do you mean?"

"Like, letters," I said. "You know. In the mail."

"You don't have a phone?"

I knew where she was coming from with that, but I was now on the other side of the argument. "Of course, we have a phone," I said. "But my aunt says sometimes words just mean more when you write them."

She looked at me for a moment. "What are you going to write?"

"I don't know," I said. "Hi and stuff."

"Hi and stuff," she repeated. "That's going to mean more in a letter?"

"Look," I said, "just write down your address for me, and I'll write you."

Joni stood straight and crossed her arms, staring at me.

"You don't believe me?" I asked.

"No, I don't."

"I promise I'll write to you."

"Am I supposed to write you back?"

"I think that's the idea, yeah," I said. I watched as the wheels turned in her head.

"I tell you what," she said, grabbing an order slip and a pen. She pushed them to me on the counter and said, "Write down your address. I'll write to you. Then you'll have my address. If you write me back, we can take it from there."

I could tell her idea wasn't up for debate, so I wrote down my name and address and slid it back to her.

"Now, what flavor snowball can I get you?"

"I've spent all my money," I admitted. "I'm broke."

She put her hands on her hips, pretending to be serious, and said, "How are you going to buy stamps for all my letters if you don't have any money?"

"I'll get a job," I said, only half-joking. "I'll work for my dad at his coffee shop."

"All right," she said. "I'll make you an orange snowball. But you owe me a dime. And I know where you live now, so…"

"I'll pay you back next summer."

"I hope so," she said, giving me a smile to remember.

THIRTY

Beautiful Sunday

I had trouble sleeping my last night at the beach. Everything I knew in Columbia – my home, my friends, my school – seemed a million miles away. And the Ran that lived there seemed like a different kid than the one lying in bed at the beach staring at the ceiling fan. I rolled over and looked out my window into the darkness. The image of a girl walking down the street in the early morning light played through my mind. But unlike that first morning, the street was empty. I rolled back over and began to dread my ride home.

With the sky's early light slowly illuminating my room, I decided to head down to the beach for one last sunrise. Joni said she wouldn't be out there, but maybe she'd change her mind and surprise me. I snuck through the den without waking anyone and crept quietly down the front stairs to the street. Just for old times' sake, I took the path past Mr. Wilson's house up and over the dunes. And I only stepped on one sandspur.

Trotting down the beach side of the dunes, it was quickly obvious that I was alone. It was much earlier than my other predawn visits, so I had some time to kill before the sun came up. With the tide about halfway up the beach, I walked along the water line all the way to the creek at the north end. Judging from the direction of the current, the tide was going out, which, according to Joni, was the best time for sharks' tooth hunting.

I drifted along aimlessly through the puddles left by the tide, hoping to find something worth keeping. Moving the sand around with my toes, I managed to find a small, black, dagger-shaped tooth. It was OK, but not what I was looking for. I also found a whole, undamaged, dead crab, just like the live one I pulled from the crab trap with Joey. I picked it up and carried it with me as I looked for more teeth. Maybe Aunt Sarah could cook something with it for breakfast. Crab and eggs and grits!

The sun was just beginning to climb over the horizon into a cloudless sky when I saw a dark triangle shape in a small pool just ahead of me. I stepped closer and bent down, assuming it was just a shell. But it wasn't just a shell. It was a perfect, one-inch, gray shark's tooth sitting on display all by itself below six inches of clear water just for me. I looked around quickly to make sure it wasn't some gag Joey was pulling on me. But I was still all alone on the beach. I picked it up and placed it in the center of my hand. As I stared at my prize, I felt a smile spread across my face. I only wished Joni was with me to see it.

With my tooth and crab in hand, I scurried back down the beach and headed for the house. I hurried up the stairs to the porch, but neither Aunt Sarah nor Uncle Breland were up, yet. I opened the refrigerator and placed my crab carefully on a shelf for safekeeping until my aunt could cook it. I returned to my room, closed the door, and lay on my bed admiring my tooth. I wondered how old it was. Maybe it was from a prehistoric shark. And maybe the shark lost it eating a little caveman kid. After a few more minutes of daydreaming about sharks and cavemen, I heard Aunt Sarah in the kitchen. Before I could get off my bed, I heard her scream. Afraid that she had hurt herself, I jumped off the bed and opened my door. Aunt Sarah stood before me holding my crab.

"Ran, honey, did you put this in my refrigerator?"

"Yes, ma'am," I said. "I thought you could make something with it."

"Where did you get it?"

"I found it on the beach this morning."

"Was it dead when you found it?"

"Oh, yes, ma'am," I said, trying to reassure her. "I wouldn't put a live crab in your refrigerator."

She closed her eyes and smiled. "That's very thoughtful of you," she said. "Why don't you take this back down to the beach? Or, better yet, take it to the creek and toss it in the marsh so the birds can eat it." She handed me the crab, then turned to wash her hands in the sink.

"You don't want to cook it?" I asked.

"We don't know how long it's been dead, honey. Next time you come to visit we'll get some fresh crab, and I'll cook something fun for you. OK?"

"OK," I said.

"What's all the fuss in here?" Uncle Breland said, entering the kitchen. He was wearing church clothes. A sport coat, a tie, and everything. He'd even combed his hair. "What's that smell?"

"Oh, Ran just left a little surprise for me in the fridge, that's all," said Aunt Sarah. She turned to me and said, "Now, run take care of that, and come right back. We're all going to church this morning."

"Yes, ma'am," I said, scooting past Uncle Breland.

"Is that a crab he's got in his hand?" I heard him ask as I hurried through the porch and down the stairs.

I jogged over to the creek, threw the crab as far as I could into the marsh grass, and hurried back to the house. I didn't bring any church clothes to the beach, so I wasn't sure what I was supposed to wear. But Aunt Sarah ironed one of my t-shirts and a pair of my shorts for me while I ate a bowl of cereal. When I finished, I got dressed and stuffed my new shark's tooth in my pocket for safekeeping.

We got in my aunt's car, instead of the truck, and I sat in the back, behind Aunt Sarah. Uncle Breland drove us, but after he backed onto the street, he went north instead of south like we normally do to leave the island.

"Where are we going?" I asked.

Aunt Sarah turned her head and said, "Ms. Mary's going with us this morning."

Uncle Breland said, "I think what you mean is, *I'm* going with you and Mary this morning."

Aunt Sarah chuckled and explained, "Ms. Mary is who I usually go to church with. We have breakfast at the diner and then go to the early service."

We pulled up to the trailer, and Ms. Mary came out. She carried her Bible and a little white purse. She wore a dress and white boots that almost came up to her knees. She got into the backseat, behind Uncle Breland.

"Hello, Ran," she said, giving me a smile.

"Hi," I said.

"Morning Mary," said Aunt Sarah, turning around to greet her.

Mary nodded at Sarah, then looked at the rearview mirror and said, "Morning, Bree."

"Morning, Mary," said Uncle Breland, looking into the mirror. "It's good to see you."

"It's good to see you too," she said.

We rode along for a few minutes without anyone talking. Ms. Mary would look at me and offer a smile without saying anything. Aunt Sarah just looked straight ahead while Uncle Breland focused on driving. I hadn't seen Ms. Mary since I took her the pie, so I asked her, "Did you finish the apple pie?"

"I did! I ate every bite. That was sweet of you to bring it over to me."

"I would have stayed and eaten more," I said, "but I had a date."

She laughed. "A date? Wow, they start young nowadays, don't they Sarah."

"Oh, yes," my aunt said.

"Was this your girlfriend?"

"No," I said. "Well, I thought she was, but she wasn't. Aunt Sarah kind of helped me see that."

"Your aunt Sarah's a smart woman," Mary said. "You listen to her, and she'll keep you out of trouble."

"I believe it," I said.

Mary and Aunt Sarah then started talking about ladies who had come into the beauty parlor. They did that all the way to Murrells Inlet where the church was. Uncle Breland stayed quiet the whole way.

The church was just off Highway 17, about halfway to the water park. I had only been inside one church my whole life, so

I was curious to see what it was like. It was made of wood instead of brick, and it looked smaller than our church at home. But there were cars parked all around it. Once inside, it seemed about the same. Rows of wooden pews, divided by a center aisle, and a stage up front with a choir sitting behind it. We sat on the right side about halfway to the front. I sat in between my aunt and Ms. Mary. When everyone stood up to sing the first hymn, someone tapped me on my shoulder. I turned around, and the man behind me stepped aside and pointed to Joni, standing two rows behind us. She waved with a big smile on her face. I realized I had never seen her with regular clothes on. She was wearing a pink dress, and her hair was in a ponytail. She looked pretty. I waved and then turned back around. I wished I didn't know she was behind me. I felt self-conscious the whole service, knowing she was looking at the back of my head.

After we sang a couple of hymns and everyone sat down, the preacher stood up and said how happy he was to have everyone there and asked if visitors would please stand so people could greet them after the service. I looked at Uncle Breland, and he shook his head at me. So, I stayed seated. Aunt Sarah patted my knee. A few seconds later, the man behind me tapped my shoulder with an offering envelope. I took it and turned it over to find a handwritten note. It simply said, "Scaredy cat!" I imagined Joni laughing at me two rows back, but I was afraid to turn around.

I felt like I needed to respond to her note in some way, so I reached into my pocket and pulled out my shark's tooth. I placed it in the envelope, licked the flap, and closed it. Under Joni's comment, I wrote, "Keep this for me until next summer." I turned around and handed it back to the man behind me, who seemed to be enjoying his role as our go-between. I waited a moment and then turned my head to see Joni. She had the biggest smile on her face I'd seen all summer.

After the service finally ended, I stood up and looked behind me. Joni waved and said, "Hey," and I did the same. But we couldn't talk with the crowd filing out between us. Then several people came up to speak to Uncle Breland, and I kept getting introduced to them. As all that was happening, I kept my eyes on Joni, as she and her family slowly made their way down the aisle and out the door. It was the last time I saw her that summer.

THIRTY-ONE

Seasons in the Sun

The very first time I rode a bicycle all by myself came as a bit of a surprise. Up until then, once the training wheels had come off, my dad would run behind me, holding the back of my seat while I pedaled. This allowed me to have all the fun of riding a bike without worrying about things like gravity. On that particular day, we were heading down a slight hill in our neighborhood. I was talking about something I thought was funny and laughing while I pedaled. When I didn't hear my dad laugh, I turned my head and looked for him. There he was, at the top of the hill, a hundred yards behind me. He stood waving his arm over his head, smiling. I immediately crashed.

He came running down the hill, the smile still on his face as I sat next to my bike crying. "You did it!" he said, repeatedly. "That was great! You see? You don't need me! You can do it all by yourself!"

From that time on, I rode my bike without my dad.

After church, we dropped Ms. Mary off at her trailer. Uncle Breland got out and walked her to her door. They talked for a minute or two, then hugged each other before she went inside. When he got back in the car, Aunt Sarah put her hand on his shoulder as we backed out onto the street. I didn't really understand all that was happening, but I could tell something had changed.

Once back at the house, Aunt Sarah told me to get my things together before we ate lunch, so I'd be ready when my mom got there. I went into my room and pushed everything into a pile with my feet, which I then divided evenly between my pillow case and my duffle bag. Just like that, I was ready to go home.

Aunt Sarah had asked what I wanted for lunch, and since my crab was in the marsh, I opted for a peanut butter and banana sandwich. Uncle Breland asked for the same thing, but Aunt Sarah made herself a PB&J since we used up all the bananas. I asked if we could eat on the porch, so we took our sandwiches and rocked in our chairs while we ate.

"Ran, have you enjoyed your stay with us?" Aunt Sarah asked.

It took me a few chews to be able to speak, but I finally said, "Yes, ma'am."

"Well, we've certainly enjoyed having you here," she said. "You're welcome to come back anytime."

"Ran, I should tell you," said Uncle Breland, "I've got a surprise coming your way."

"What is it?"

"If I told you, it wouldn't be a surprise. Now, would it?"

He was nicer and clean-shaven, but he was still Uncle Breland. "No, sir," I said, wondering what it could be. Was it something to do with the bike? Or fishing? Maybe he was going to pay me for cleaning Ms. Mary's yard two months ago.

As I sat thinking and finishing my sandwich, I saw a car that looked like my dad's coming down the street. It slowed and turned into the dirt parking space next to Uncle Breland's truck. I looked at my uncle. He grinned but said nothing.

I watched my dad climb out of the car, stretch his legs, and look up at the porch. "Surprise!" he said, extending his arms.

I looked back at Uncle Breland. "I told you," he said.

"Hey, Tom!" said Aunt Sarah.

"Hey, Sarah!" my dad said as he started up the stairs.

We all stood from our chairs as he came onto the porch. He gave Aunt Sarah a hug first. Then he pulled me close and squeezed the air out of me.

"Hey, sport!"

"Hey, Dad. Where's Mom?"

He laughed and said, "Where's Mom? I drive two hours to come get you and you say, 'Where's Mom?'"

He released me and extended his hand to Uncle Breland. "Hey, Brother," he said shaking hands.

"Good to see you, Tom," said my uncle.

"Thanks again for your letter," my dad told him. "It meant a lot."

Aunt Sarah elbowed me. "See?" she whispered with a wink.

"I just thought you should know," said Uncle Breland.

My dad turned to me. "So, how was your summer, kiddo?"

"It was good. I learned how to drive and how to fish and how to find sharks' teeth and—"

"Woah! Let's back up to the driving," said my dad, turning to Uncle Breland.

"It's nothing to get worried about, Tom. He did great."

"And we went to the water park too," I said.

"Wow, you have had a good time, haven't you?"

"Tom," said Aunt Sarah, "he's got all his things ready to go in his room. Don't you, Ran?"

"Yes, ma'am."

"Can I make you some lunch?" Aunt Sarah asked my dad.

"Oh, no thanks, Sarah. I had something in the car on the way down."

My dad put his hand on my shoulder and said, "Why don't we go for a quick walk on the beach before we get in the car? What do you say?"

"OK," I said. While I was happy and surprised to see my dad, I started to get the feeling that something was going on. There was the letter from Uncle Breland. My stay getting cut short by a week. And then my dad actually taking a day off from the café when my mom could've picked me up. I may have been twelve, but I wasn't blind. And now the walk on the beach? I was definitely in some kind of trouble.

Once we got on the street, I steered us toward the public beach access. The beach was fairly crowded. Some high school kids had set up a volleyball net about halfway toward the pier, and they were playing a game. Other than that, it was just the usual weekend scattering of moms in beach chairs and little kids digging holes. We turned left and began walking in the wet sand toward the north end.

"Son," my dad began, "I know you weren't happy with me about being sent down here for the summer. Your mom told me how you felt."

"She did?"

"Hm-mm. We talked a lot about it. But I want you to know my reasons for doing that."

"OK."

"I was thinking of both you and your uncle Breland. We never told you about Bobby, but you know about that now, right?"

"Yes, sir."

"Well, when your uncle lost Bobby, he never got over it. He was never the same. And he got a little hard to be around. You know what I mean?"

"Yes, sir. He's always been kind of scary to me."

"I know. He was hurting. And then his first marriage failed too."

"To Ms. Mary."

"That's right."

"She went to church with us today," I said.

"Mary did?! Was Breland with you?"

"Yes, sir."

"Oh, my gosh. Wow! This is better than I hoped for."

"What did you hope for?"

"Son, I've been trying to help your uncle deal with his grief over Bobby since you were born. As a matter of fact, when your mom and I had you, it only made things worse for him. And he resented you."

"What did I do?"

"You didn't do anything. But you came along just a short time after Bobby drowned. And your uncle just couldn't be happy for me."

"Is that why he's always called me names and made fun of me?"

"Probably. I've tried talking to him, calling him. I've written him letters. But I just couldn't get through to him."

"So, why did you send me to stay with him if you knew he didn't like me?"

"Because I believed he needed you. You being here forced him to deal with some things I don't think he would have otherwise. I'm sorry to put you in the middle of that, but I didn't know what else to do. Besides, I felt like you needed him too."

"I needed Uncle Breland?"

"Son, I know I haven't been there for you the past few years. And I thought—"

"Dad, it's OK. You've got the coffee shop. I get it."

My dad stayed quiet for a moment as we walked. "Ran," he finally said, "do you know why I opened the café in the first place?"

"Because you love coffee," I said, stating the obvious.

"No, I don't even drink coffee."

"What?" I said in disbelief.

He stopped and faced me. "Son, listen to me for a moment. Before I started third grade in Columbia, do you know how many times my dad had moved us?"

"No," I said, unaware they had moved at all or what that had to do with his anti-coffee confession.

"Four times," he said.

"Really?" I asked.

"Really, four times," he said. "And it was hard on us. Probably harder on your uncle than me because he was older. It was always new schools and new friends."

"That would stink," I said, beginning to empathize a bit.

"Son, I opened the café so you would never have to worry about all that. You could have one place to call home. One set of friends to grow up with. The café was my way of making sure of that. Does that make sense?" he asked, starting to walk again.

"I guess," I said, walking along beside him. "But what good is all that if you're never around?"

"Well, that's been the problem," he said with a nod of his head. "To make the café work, I've had to give a lot more of myself than I ever imagined. And it's cost me a lot of time with you and your mom. And I'm sorry about that."

I looked up at him. My dad saying he was sorry was something I wasn't expecting. And I could tell he really meant it. But there was still the question of my summer of exile. "OK, but what does all that have to do with me coming to the beach?"

"Ran, you're almost thirteen."

"In two weeks," I reminded him.

"That's right. You'll be a teenager in two weeks. And with everything I have going on with the café, I can't always be there for you. We both know that. That means you're going to have to figure out a few things on your own, without me. This summer was a time for you to do that. I wanted you to have something I couldn't give you."

I realized then just what I had been given over the last two months. "A summer to remember," I heard myself say.

"That's right," he said, smiling. "Like your mom always says, 'Summers are a gift.'"

We said that together. My mom would have liked that.

We walked on for a moment without talking. I needed to rethink things. I had believed all summer that my dad just wanted to get rid of me. That I was something he'd rather not have to worry about. That he loved coffee more than me. But it seemed I was wrong about everything.

"What did Uncle Breland say in his letter?" I asked.

"Well, for starters, he told me what a fine young man you are. He's really grown fond of you since you got here. He also told me I should be spending more time with my son." He smiled and put his hand on my shoulder.

"Is that why you came to get me?"

He nodded. "We talked on the phone after I got his letter. Me coming instead of your mom was his idea, and I thought it was a good one. He also said you helped him become friends with Frank Wilson, again."

"Mr. Wilson's been fishing with us a lot the last few weeks."

"That's amazing. You just don't know how big a change that is for your uncle. And church with Mary. Wow."

"Why does Ms. Mary live in that little trailer?"

"She still lives there?"

"Yes, sir. I had to clean her yard."

"Your uncle put you to work, huh?"

"Yes, sir. So, why does she live there?"

"Well, after she and your uncle divorced, let's just say Mary made some bad choices. She married again and got divorced again. Then she got involved with the wrong people. She lost everything. Your uncle had to physically pull her out of a bad situation and put her in his camper. He moved it onto the island so he could keep an eye on her. And your aunt Sarah has been like a sister to Mary over the years."

"Ms. Mary's a nice lady."

"She is. And I'm thinking she and Breland might finally be getting on with their lives. And a lot of that is because of you, according to Uncle Breland's letter."

"But I didn't do anything."

"You were here, Son. That's all it took."

I looked up at my dad as he walked beside me. "So, you set this whole summer up on purpose?" I asked.

"Pretty much," he said. "Are you still mad at me?"

I had learned a lot over the summer. One thing was knowing when you're in a good position to negotiate. So, I asked, "Can I come back next year?"

My dad laughed and said, "Of course, you can come back next summer."

Suddenly, the next nine months had purpose. We turned around and started back toward the house.

"Dad?"

"Yeah, Son?"

"Can I work for you at the coffee shop?"

"Why, sure! I'd love that, man!"

"Just after school, I mean. I need to save some money for stamps."

EPILOGUE

From seventh grade through high school, I spent every summer with Aunt Sarah and Uncle Breland. He eventually got his TV working again, but we rarely turned it on. Over that time, Joey became a regular fishing buddy of my uncle and Mr. Wilson, even when I wasn't there. Joni and I exchanged letters during each school year and hung out together at King's each summer. And, yes, she did embarrass me at putt-putt several times. But it took a long time before we called ourselves a couple. We each saw other people from time to time. The summer before my senior year of high school, I actually had a dinner date with Heather. It ended early.

To further complicate matters, Joni went to Clemson. I stayed in Columbia and studied at the University of South Carolina. But we never fell out of touch. By our junior years, we were finally an item, albeit a long-distance one. After my first year of law school, we were married in her church at the beach, ten summers after we met. At our reception, we had our caterer serve a custom Italian dish, combining risotto, meatballs, and ravioli. We labeled it "Ranjoni." And I gave a toast to my mom, stating publicly that she was indeed right. Love takes time.

My dad and I learned how to spend time together, even if it was on his terms. I worked with him in the café for eight years, all the way through college. I got to know and appreciate my dad, and for that I'm thankful. After he passed away last year, I sold his coffee shop. The new owner changed the name to The Lost Bean, so if you're ever in Columbia, you should stop by.

This morning, my wife and I decided to take our three-year-old son, Tommy, out on the beach for his first sunrise. It's the Fourth of July, the Monday of our annual vacation week, and he woke us up early. Uncle Breland, Sarah, and my mom were still asleep upstairs; at least we didn't hear the floor creaking above us. Joey and his wife hadn't come out of their room yet, either. So, we snuck out down the hall through the porch, making sure the screen door didn't slam closed behind us. We had just made it to the street when we heard Sarah from her rocking chair on the porch upstairs.

"Joni, would y'all like some blueberry pancakes when you get back?"

"That would be wonderful, yes, ma'am!" Joni said.

Aunt Sarah was still Aunt Sarah, even in her late sixties.

With each of us holding one of Tommy's hands, we hurried over what was left of the dunes beside Mr. Wilson's old house. The sun was just edging over the horizon.

"Look, Tommy!" said Joni. "The sun's coming up."

Tommy was too preoccupied to look up, watching a fiddler crab slowly back away in front of him. Maybe three is a little too young to care about sunrises, but it did get us all on the beach. And since we were out there, we began a slow walk on the sand, just enjoying the morning together.

"Look, Daddy, baby turtles!" said Tommy, pointing.

From a nest below the dunes came a stream of freshly hatched baby sea turtles. Fortunately, the tide wasn't too far out, so they didn't have far to go. Several people had stopped to watch and guard their progress toward the ocean.

"Where's the momma?" asked Tommy.

"The momma leaves her eggs here on the beach and then goes back into the ocean," I explained.

"Why does she do that?" asked Tommy.

"Well, it's nature's way of making them stronger," I said. "So, when they hatch and are on their own, they'll have a better chance at survival."

Joni leaned against me and slipped her hand into mine. "Sounds like another sea turtle I know," she said, kissing me on the cheek.

ABOUT THE AUTHOR

Greg M. Dodd lives in Columbia, South Carolina with his wife, Caroline, and their two dogs. He earned both his bachelor's and master's degrees from the University of South Carolina. Greg's debut novel, *A Seed for the Harvest*, won a Silver Medal for Christian Fiction in the 2015 Illumination Book Awards. His second novel, *The Gills Creek Five*, won three literary book awards in 2017. His other published works include the short stories *Letters from Damascus* and *The Lost Bean*, as well as a contribution to the anthology *Precious, Precocious Moments* (compiled by Yvonne Lehman). Readers may visit Greg's website, gregmdodd.com, to stay current with news regarding his works.

Made in the USA
Middletown, DE
23 November 2023

43204116R00142